The Anomalies

a novel by

Joey Goebel

MacAdam/Cage Publishing
155 Sansome Street, Suite 550
San Francisco, CA 94104
www.macadamcage.com
Copyright © 2003 by Joey Goebel
ALL RIGHTS RESERVED

Library of Congress Cataloging-in-Publication Data

Goebel, Joey, 1980—
The anomalies / Joey Goebel.
p. cm.
ISBN 1-931561-29-X(Hardcover : alk. paper)
1. Alienation (Social psychology)—Fiction. 2. City and town life—
Fiction. 3. Prejudices—Fiction. 4. Kentucky—Fiction. I. Title.
PS3607.O33A56 2002
813'.6—dc21

2002156080

Manufactured in the United States of America
10 9 8 7 6 5 4 3 2 1

Book design by Dorothy Carico Smith.

The Anomalies

a novel by

Joey Goebel

MacAdam/Cage

Dedicated in loving memory to
Adam Joseph Goebel Jr.

CONTENTS

"I could have been someone..."
"Well, so could anyone."

—The Pogues

I. Human Potential

Luster

It wasn't easy simultaneously mending six billion broken hearts, but I managed.

That is the first line of the book that I am going to write someday. It will be the best book ever, based on my life story, wiser than all tabloids and sexier than the Bible. Oprah will approve.

This very bedroom will be blocked off by velvet ropes, and the carpet stains will become collector's items sold on eBay. And when they who hail from where the phone books are thicker see my humble origins, they'll all be thinking the same thought:

"How is it that while cell phones were ringing show tunes, while anxiety disorders were going airborne, while the world was getting so heavy that gravity got redundant, there existed a malnourished boy slashing out such valuable, world-changing thoughts that would later become our anthems, jotting out a revolution per minute in spiral notebooks on a maggot-filled bed in a musty bedroom in a grotesque home on an illiterate street in an incestuous town in such a sad, sad state?"

I ask myself the same question with the answer hovering behind me reeking of malt liquor and marijuana. He's forcing some greatness out of me, this man, this horribly average humanoid.

He taunts me. "You're so smart, you know whum

sayin. Then write me one of your stupid songs, you smart-ass, bitch-ass bitch."

With his big gun pressed against the back of my mind, he inspires me. And so I spit out some lyrics as he cocks the gun like the true Neanderthal he is.

II. That's What They All Say

Opal

You hear people talking about wavelengths. I reckon I have one of those wavelengths that's hard to pick up on. Maybe I'm still on AM or something. I don't know. But there are a few hearing me, like this one I got in the passenger's seat spitting hawkers at the pedestrians. They think she's cute 'til they have a wad of her venom running down the side of their face. Then she's not so much cute as she is disgusting. I think they feel the same way about me.

I am ten times as old as Ember, but we're still on about the same level. Either she's really mature, or I'm really immature. I don't know. I guess the biggest difference between us (besides the seventy-two years) is that I love boys, and she hates 'em. But that will change.

"You know what, girlfriend?" I say to my little bitty buddy as she's trying to generate her some more spit. "You and me are a lot alike."

"No, we're not."

"Yes, we are! We hate being bored, and we're always restless, and I sure am glad I socialize with someone like you instead of eating early-bird breakfasts at Hardee's and playing in those bridge tournaments all the time."

"I'm glad I don't watch bullshit Disney cartoons," she replies.

"That's right," I say. "You don't care about those cereal box doodads that the other kids like, either."

We jump out of my station wagon and I take off that stupid velour sweatsuit as quickly as I can. I never let Ember's parents see me in my rock clothes, just in case they care. I really doubt they do. They seem to be getting less and less interested in their kid and more and more interested in their theme parties and vacations to islands I've never heard of.

After I throw my old lady costume in the back seat, Ember and I race each other to the door of the Red Lobster, which she picked. She loves their mahi-mahi. I told her Luster won't like a chain restaurant, but she didn't care. I can't complain, though, because I love their chicken fingers.

Of course, those little legs of hers beat my arthritic ass to the restaurant.

Hostess

For the first time tonight, I mean my smile. I can't help it. There's a little girl, like, about seven or eight years old, and she's skipping toward me, and her skipping is kind of in time with the Muzak. I swear...she's an angel.

She's got curly blonde hair, a baby face, and the biggest, prettiest eyes. She kind of looks like that girl off those old Welch's grape juice commercials, only not as creepy. Her parents have got her dressed skanky, though. She's got on a T-shirt with a monster truck on it, Gravedigger. It's way too big for her and comes down past her knees. It looks like she's not even wearing any pants, which I've always thought was such a tacky look for a kid. She's got cute shoes on, at least. Black and white saddle oxfords.

"Hi!" I say to her.

"Hey."

She looks behind her at an old lady walking toward us, probably her grandma. The grandma makes me smile even more, and I'm biting my lip, trying not to laugh. She has short but really poofy white hair and wears bun-tight blue jeans, black tasseled cowboy boots, and a T-shirt that says "Sex Pistols" on it. I can't think of what celebrity she looks like, probably because there aren't any celebrities that are old ladies.

"Hi! How many? Two?"

Then in a loud, high-pitched, old lady voice, the grandma goes, "No. Five. The others will arrive shortly."

So I ask for a name, like I'm supposed to.

"Oglesby."

I ask for a smoking preference, like I'm supposed to. But this time, the high-pitched voice comes from the adorable little girl.

"Smoking!"

And I finally get an excuse to laugh. I'm told to compliment the customers as much as possible, but I mean it this time.

"Your granddaughter is *so* cute."

"She's not my granddaughter," says the old lady. "And I ain't no mammaw."

Ember

The dumbass hostess sits us down. Everybody here is dumb. Except for Opal and me. We like rock music. We rock out.

There are some families with moms and dads. There are men and women on dates. And there are some pretty-boys. That's who's here.

A waiter comes up to us. I see Opal looking at him the way she looks at wrestlers.

"Hi! My name is Todd, and I'll be your server. What can I get you two to drink?"

"Michelob Light," I tell him.

"Oh! Your granddaughter is *so* cute!"

"She's not my granddaughter," says Opal. "And I ain't no mammaw."

And I wasn't trying to be cute.

"Oh. I'm sorry," says our fuckface waiter.

"I'll take a Vervifontaine, and give her a Shirley Temple instead of that Michelob."

I don't want a Shirley Temple. I would normally be screaming by now. But I like Opal. So I'll hold off.

"I'm sorry," says Shit-head. "We don't have Vervi– what you just said."

No place ever has what she wants.

"Okay. Just Budweiser me, then," says Opal.

"Okay. Thanks. I'll have those right out," says Assface. Opal keeps busy looking at the waiter's butt. So I play with my knife. Mutilate. Mootilate. I'm getting good at not cutting myself.

"Now don't you cut off those purdy little fingers, Ember."

I point the knife at her.

"Ohhh. Don't hurt me, now, or the Boogie-man will come and get you."

"Shit. I'll cut his ass, too."

I've never been afraid of the Boogie-man. Because there is no Boogie-man. There's no Boogie-man. There's no Tooth Fairy. There's no Easter Bunny. And there is especially no Santa Claus. I'm not stupid. Santa Claus is a big, fat lie used to keep kids in line.

I hate the holidays.

Waiter

I wanna bone this chick.

She rolls in with some big, goofy-looking black dude. I'm thinking they're not a couple because they don't look right together. He has, like, big Jheri-curled hair and wears a T-shirt with a poodle on it and bleach-streaked blue jeans and white dress shoes. He kind of looks like the black dude off *Saturday Night Live* but with no facial hair.

Meanwhile, she's white. Creamy white. She's got long black hair and wears a tight white dress and fishnets. She's got the perfect amount of make-up and the perfect amount of cleavage. She kind of looks like that girl off of *Baywatch* only prettier and realer. Too bad she's in a wheelchair. Still, though, I don't care. She could give me a blow job, if nothing else, and you know I'm all about blow jobs.

What's really weird is that the hostess I boned takes the wheelchair chick and the black dude to the table with the weird old lady and the weird little girl that's not her grandkid.

I approach the table again.

"Hi! My name is Todd, and I'll be your server. What can I get you two to drink?"

I try not to look at the hot chick's boobs, but I fail. Damn.

"I'll have a Hawaiian Punch." She sounds soft and breathy like Marilyn Monroe.

"I'm sorry. We don't have Hawaiian Punch."

"Then I'll just have a root beer."

"I'm sorry. We don't have root beer, either." Boobs.

"Water."

"Okay. And for you, sir?"

"I would like to drink a glass of Coca-Cola Classic, please." He doesn't talk like a black guy, or a white guy, for that matter. He e-nun-ci-ates each syllable like he thinks I'm stupid or that I have a hearing problem or something.

"Is Pepsi okay?" I am supposed to ask every time, just in case. Then he stares me down like I just made fun of his mama or something.

"No! No, it is not okay, you jumping-to-conclusions mother fletcher! Just bring me milk!"

"Okay. Thanks. I'll have those right out."

Dude. Good thing I asked.

Ray

People work there. People eat there also. I walk in, wanting to buy food and eat it publicly. A girl at work there smiles a big one at me. I smile one back and walk quickly toward the eating. Making her yell at me.

"Wait! Sir, how many?" I hear before I can reach the

eating room.

I turn around to the girl.

"I don't understand."

"How many are in your party?"

I stare at her, thinking, flipping through my mind. Parties. How many.

"How many people do you plan to eat with?" she asks in a slow, loud voice like I am a retard baby. I hold up four.

"Smoking or non?" she asks.

I think with care before answering.

"I don't understand."

"Sir, do you like smoking cigarettes, or would you prefer not to be around anyone who *does* like smoking cigarettes?"

And then I remember how you have so many choices here. They separate eaters by their smoking here. I love this! But I just want to eat.

"I prefer being around a young black man, a little girl, an elderly woman, and a pretty girl in a wheelchair."

The girl smiles.

"Oh. Okay. I think I *might* know which table you're talking about."

She wants to laugh but holds it. She thinks I don't see the humor in this situation.

Customer

Just when I thought things couldn't get any freakier, this pudgy gay-looking middle-aged foreigner comes in. This dude is flamin, prancin in wearing flip-flops with white socks, *really* short khaki shorts, a cut-off shirt, and a denim fanny pack. Plus a big black mustache. Otherwise he's your typical dark-skinned Middle Eastern–looking dude, but with no beard and no towel on his head. He sits next to the old lady wearing the shirt that says "Sex Pistols" on it.

"Guys, I never thought I'd see this day," I say to my boys. "We are no longer at the cool table." They laugh. I kick ass.

So I'm thinking this must be like a field trip from wherever they keep crazy or retarded people or something. Shit. There's gotta be some explanation for them to be together like that. Who's gonna show up next? A rabbi? A midget? A robot?

My boys and I continue to watch them as we finish off our Rolling Rocks. The little girl almost lights herself a cigarette before the old bitch takes it away from her and smokes it herself. This must have reminded Josh and Jeremy to light up, so I light up also.

"I've never seen so many bad haircuts at one table," I tell my boys. Another laugh. I love it.

That one bitch is hot, though. Too bad she's in a wheelchair, 'cause I'm sure by the way she looks that she's a major ho. The little girl will probably be hot someday. I bet the old bitch was hot like seventy years ago.

Dude. I swear the wheelchair slut is looking over here. She's all over my stick.

Josh's cell phone rings to the tune of an old Jay-Z song, the one where he samples from that song off of *Annie*. This should be the call we've been waiting on from Josh's dealer, Jerome. My wife should be putting the kid and herself to bed in a couple hours, freeing up the crib for my boys and me to party in later. I think I'll ask that hostess that I boned in high school to come party with us.

"I bet that group really knows how to party," I say to my boys. Not a huge laugh, but I'm still the man. I laugh really loud at myself to compensate.

Then the black guy suddenly turns around, so we kind of stop laughing and look the other way to be polite.

Aurora

If I had eyes in place of nipples, I'd be losing a staring contest right now. But at least I'm not the only one they're gawking at. My friends divert some of the stares, which is one more reason to remain friends with them.

"Ooh! Let's make a toast!" I suggest after the waiter brings Ray his Mountain Dew. I've recently become fond of toasting because it's one of those things you can do to make yourself feel more grown-up without spreading disease.

"Yeah. Good thinking," says Luster. "What should we toast to, little Ember?"

"Vaginas."

"I like that. To vaginas," says Luster.

And we all raise our glasses and say "to vaginas," which I'm not too comfortable with.

I'm at an awkward age and have been for nineteen years. And it keeps getting worse. For instance, at my dad's parties, there's the problem of talking to his friends. Numerically, I am old enough now to be expected to carry on conversations with them, but I never know what to say, and I always end up feeling dumb. Sometimes I think I should be like my sister the slut and move to California. Then I wouldn't have to deal with things like my dad's parties.

At least I don't have to worry about feeling dumb here, though. I can say whatever comes to mind.

"Your hair looks flippindicular, Opal," I say. It has been freshly permed.

"I know. I just got it done today," she replies.

"I was thinking about going back to blonde, but black goes better with the whole Satan thing," I say.

She simply nods. I'm accepted here, and I'm actually happy to be around these people. I see these friends as being like the vending machines in the basement of a hospital.

Back when my mom was dying, and Dad and my sister the slut and I would visit the hospital, the only source of pleasure or escape I could find there were the vending machines in the basement. Everything else was sick or sanitized, beige and horrible, and underneath such unflattering lights. But then there were the vending machines in the basement, full of happy, colorful packages, just like you'd find them outside the hospital.

As I've gotten older, candy doesn't even taste as good as it used to, but that's beside the point. The point is that I am capable of coming up with metaphors.

At this point, I am positive that those guys are staring at us. I know this type of guy from high school, and although they look to be in their early twenties, I'm sure their mentalities never made it past the twelfth grade. These were the guys that would cut in front of everyone in the lunch line as if it were their divine right to eat before the lesser people. These are the guys that had to be on the front row for the senior class picture so everyone could see them flipping off the camera (how rebellious!). These are the guys that rode with their windows down playing rap, always driving with the exact same pose, their left elbow resting on the door, their left hand coolly draped over their mouth, almost as if they were posing for a senior picture. I didn't want any part of them then, and I don't want any part of them now. That's why I refuse to go to college, to avoid being around young people.

And they're looking at my friends and me and laughing.

"They're *still* doing it," I say. "I get so sick of this."

"It is a sad occasion when laughter is not welcome. If this continues, I *will* confront their asses," says Luster.

"No, Luster, please. Not again." I change the subject. "So what did you learn in school today, Ember? And don't say 'nothing.'"

"I skipped school today."

"Yes!" exclaims Ray. "I thought I saw you riding your dirt bike past tanning bed, but I had a customer and couldn't greet you one."

Even as he speaks, I notice Ray looking all around the restaurant, trying to find his man.

Then the well-dressed males with their Jason Priestley smiles and boy band facial hair share another loud giggle blatantly directed toward our table, and it is Ember, not Luster, who snaps.

"Shuts the hell up!" she roars, standing up on her chair, pointing her silverware at the men. "I have a knife, and I will cut you from your wooter to your tooter." I think it's a line she got from an audience member on *Jenny Jones.*

"Take it easy, kid," one of them says. "I think somebody forgot to take her Ritalin."

His idiot friends laugh at him, and Luster suddenly stands up.

"Please sit down, my rabid child," says Luster. Ember

pouts and reluctantly sits. She lays down her knife, and I take it from her, just in case. Then we listen to Luster, the spokesman of our group.

Customer

So this black guy with big, goofy hair is staring at me with a crazed look in his eyes, probably fucked up on something. I decide to play it cool for now.

"What's up, man?" I say.

"I apologize for my rambunctious dining companion. She lives like a Punky Brewster deluxe. She felt that you males were staring and laughing at us. Were you?"

"Nah, dude. We were laughing at something else. Don't worry about it."

"But I am going to worry about it. You are lying to me. It worries me that you can so easily lie like that. It also worries me that you think I am so stupid. So to quiet my mind, could you tell me why you would lie to me like that?"

"Well…Because I *can*, bro." My boys laugh. I rule.

"Is my dining party so grotesque that you would utterly disregard our feelings? Is that what you are saying to me?"

"Well, I don't know about all that, man. Hey, you can't bullshit a bullshitter." That's my slogan. That's what I always wrote in yearbooks next to my name and jersey number. "Hey—let me buy you a drink. No hard feelings, huh?"

I'm trying to be cool to this guy, but I think I just pissed him off even more. He sits down next to me.

"Oh, have a seat, why don't you?" I say.

"I want you to tell me exactly why you would stare and laugh at us," he says. "Put it in syllables."

"Dude, chill, man," says Jeremy. "We didn't mean anything—"

"Keep out of this, Hilfiger. I am talking to the man with no hard feelings."

That's me, apparently. I would like to defuse this situation before I have to kick some ass.

"Dude—"

"Do you think calling me dude first cushions what you are saying? Am I supposed to know that you are being sincere since you take the time to call me dude?"

"Dude, man—"

"Bite. I have come to expect people to laugh at our motley crew. That is a given, you jerk-wad almighty. But I would like for you to tell me exactly *why* you are laughing. Can you articulate your thoughts, or are they as empty as I think? Is there any brain in the gleams of your eyes? Does that tongue know how to whip it? Can you enlighten a man who has heard it all and has even written it all down on four-by-six index cards?"

What the fuck? I'm all about being different and all, but this dude is a trip. He's freakin me out here. He just needs to chill and hear where I'm coming from.

"Hey, man, it's nothing personal," I say.

"Nothing personal? Nothing personal? What are you going to say next? *No offense? These things happen?*"

"I don't know about all that."

"So it is nothing personal? You just randomly pick out people and ruin their evenings?"

"Nah, dawg, but like you say, you expect people to laugh at you. Just seeing all of you together like that. It just—"

Before I can finish my sentence, he starts digging around in the back of his underwear. He pulls out some notecards and throws one on the table. It says MAKES NO SENSE.

"Exactly. You read my mind."

"It takes no clairvoyance to predict a humanoid's sentence."

"Oh. So I'm a humanoid, now?"

"Yes. A humanoid is what you are. You are another pretty face in the ugly crowd. You are a cop in a doughnut shop. You are programmed to the end. You can be read from start to finish in one sitting."

"Fuck you," I say as he throws another notecard on the table. It says FUCK YOU.

"I knew you would say that. You are a stereotypical human being. You listen to typical stereo."

"Okay. Tell me what I listen to then, smart-ass."

He looks me over before answering.

"You listen to Eminem."

"Yeah. So what? Everybody listens to Eminem."

"I do not, nor do my dining companions. But I will not stop there. I can unfold your life story here before me."

I've never been in a situation like this before. This is fucked up. I don't know what to do but to listen.

Luster

You were born a mistake into a middle-class family that thought they were a high-class family. Your life was fine until your asshole parents divorced. Before that it was bike rides, baseball, swimming, and Nintendo. But after the divorce, your Nike Airs walked astray. You blamed yourself at first for your parents' split, but then you learned to blame them instead, and on them you would blame everything forevermore. As a teenager, you felt your problems at home licensed you to rebel. You partied hard and lived for the weekends. You felt obligated to lose your virginity and you did as soon as someone would help you to do so. You did just well enough in school to get by, saying that you were smart but just didn't "apply yourself." You left home as soon as possible to go to college. You joined a frat. You let females control your destiny. You accidentally got a girl pregnant and felt obligated to marry her. You wanted a boy. You got a job that you hate but it "pays the bills" as you like to say. Your wife appears not as pretty as she was when you impregnated her, and your eyes are starting to wander. You and your wife consider yourselves better than your neighbors. You are depressed. You smoke weed to help you not be. You work out. You go to a tanning bed. You worry about your hair.

After a lengthy pause, alpha-male says, "Shut up. You don't know me...I'm not depressed."

You will be. It is bound to happen sometime between your divorce from your cheating wife and when your kids put you in a nursing home.

"That's it, man. Are you done, or am I gonna have to kick your ass?"

I throw one more card on the table, the one that says EMPTY THREAT OF VIOLENCE–A FINAL RESORT. My cards never fail. I've got everything from TOO MUCH INFORMATION to I NEED CLOSURE to I ALREADY HAVE A BOYFRIEND to BAD HAIR DAY?

I am done. I am sorry for confronting you as I have in front of your peers, some of whom are secretly gay.

At this, the asshole's friends look at one another nervously.

I know how much respect means to you, and I respectfully ask that you refrain from mistreating my friends and me.

"Whatever, dude."

I return to my table. I don't like doing things like I just did, but the humanoids make it so easy for me, and the fact that they make it so easy for me is why I do it in the first place. I can predict the prettyboy just like I can predict that the guy wearing a bowtie will be a smart-ass, that the traveling children's storyteller will be annoyingly eccentric, that the English teacher will love Garrison Keillor, that the bartender will be exceedingly confident.

"Why do you always have to make a scene like that?" asks Aurora.

You were the one complaining about them staring at us. Are they staring at us *now*?

The man's friends are comforting him, patting him on the shoulder.

Then a contagiously funky reggae song comes on. My dining companions and I spontaneously arise and dance in the middle of the restaurant, except for Aurora who just rolls back and forth. We dance like protozoa, squirming unattached, our bodies moving like they don't even know it. Music, music. Muse, sick muse. The sick muse we will follow to a timeshare on the moon.

I approach my victim, the professional humanoid.

Come on, dude! No hard feelings, right!? Would you like to dance?

"Oh, shut the fuck up."

I smile, laugh, and proceed with the dancing. I dance as hard as I can since I know that any moment now, someone will tell us to stop and sit down, or more specifically, someone will tell us, *"I'm going to have to ask you to stop and sit down."*

III. The Nightmare Day

Luster

Get up. Time to rock it like a honeysuckle meter maid. Time to face the nightmare day. A lot of assholes depend on you.

Here begins my nightmare day. I am a twenty-four-year-old commissary runner at the dog-racing track. It is my duty to make sure that all the concession stands have enough alcohol and cigarettes. It is not a gratifying job, and I do not get along well with my co-workers. I have been clinically diagnosed with a busted ass, and at the end of the day, when I punch the clock, I want to punch the clock.

Of course, I am just biding my time until I become big and famous. Some call what I am doing now "paying my dues." Others call it "building character." I call it "suffering." My dream is to one day not suffer as much as I suffer now. I hope to be a rock star, a famous orator, a television personality on the Labor Day telethon, a poet, a philosopher king, a leader of men, and/or a rock star supreme. I want to rock it like Chuck Norris on the tilt-a-whirl.

Dressed in my personalized work shirt, I walk through our decrepit living room where a few of my brothers lie around naked on the floor. Despite my talking aloud to myself, they do not awaken. Jerome still seems to be passed out where I left him last night after he was done threatening to blow my brain into the hereafter.

Alone, I wait for the bus, trying not to notice that everything around me is dying the mildew death, the great cracked concrete standstill that is the case in the Midwest, a land that doesn't know whether to stay or grow, a realm that calls it quits after a Wal-Mart, a Red Lobster, and a winning basketball team, an undecided, unambitious region that ultimately ends up a halfway house for humanity, full of pointless towns and hindered sons. A god needs to drop a bomb here to improve it.

Sometimes I awake to an awful noise, and I find myself hoping that I am hearing a nuclear bomb falling on my town, on this neighborhood. I either want all of the world or nothing. Until my future arrives, I have to settle for neither. And that awful noise always ends up being gangsta rap bursting from one of my brothers' car speakers.

Passenger

That crazy black bastard with the hair is talking to himself again. He's been doing this for years, so he don't scare us no more. Used to, he'd have a whole big section of the bus to hisself 'cause we thought he was dangerous. But now, we'll sit close to him and don't even look at him when he's talking like that. It just took some getting used to, and now I think the bus would seem empty without that big black voice of his. Every once in a while, he'll say something real interesting, but most of the time, he don't make sense, like now.

"William Blake wrote, 'Without contraries is no progression.' I hold this to be true, and it may offer some insight into the magnificent splendor that is me."

He's always quoting people I never heard of. Probably rappers or basketball players or something. Whatever it is, it's stuff that has no place on a Monday morning on a southbound bus in a small Kentucky town like this here.

Luster

One half of me is a proud escapee from the science of life. I cut loose from the George Strait jacket. I am physically incapable of blushing. I am not subject to linear thought. I think in poetry. I prefer the backseat to shotgun. I apologize to insects before I kill their asses. I cannot swim, nor do I feel the need to learn.

The other half of me falls victim to the typical urges, hopes, and dreams of the humanoids. I want to be rich. I want to be big and famous. And above all, I want to love and be loved. In these ways, I am a slave like all the rest. I want to rock it like a slut with bad shoes. I want to be thigh-high in Ted Nugent nostalgia.

Like most men, I think about sex every six seconds. But unlike most men, every seventh second I think about how the girl would look wearing the burlap pantsuit that my show business money afforded her.

Without these pre-programmed urges combined with my weird-boy flair, I would stagnate. I would be condemned to living in the third world planet I call home forevermore. Without these contraries, Luster Johnson could not progress.

I believe that my funk-ass uniqueness is a virtue that will ultimately allow me to slip through some crack somewhere in order to achieve the fame, riches, and dream woman that elude so many others. I believe that my dreams will come true and everything will eventually fall into place for me. Once I have the fame and riches that allow a human to be taken seriously, then and only then will I be able to exert my inter-galactic clout in an effort to change the spin of the Earth on the axis that represses, a spin for the better, Lady Sajak. This is me being an idealist.

Robert Penn Warren wrote, "If you are an idealist, it does not matter what you do or what goes on around you because it isn't real anyway." I could not agree more.

I do not consider the humanoids to really be there. They are merely holographic projections of what they think they are supposed to be. You are what you pretend to be. And even though they are not really there, the humanoids manage to be the bane of my existence. And yet I do not like to see another human cry. And I want them to love me.

Off the bus and into work, my tightly tied shoes drag me through the petty wage days, starting me all over again at the end of a line of clock-punchers. One by one, we volunteer for another nightmare day.

Love me. Love me tenderly. I want to be loved. Perhaps my overwhelming need for love stems from growing up as the middle child in a house with 12 brothers (all named Jerome). Maybe I needed more attention and affection. Maybe I want to rock you like a mild thunderstorm.

No one has ever fallen in love with me. I think this is because I am so fucking weird. The truth is, I have nothing in common with anyone.

I now push a cart full of beer cases through the area underneath the grandstands while many of the spectators squeal above. This duty is somewhat difficult because so many idiot patrons get in my way. Most of these patrons are dirty men and look depressed because they are losing their money. When they *do* win here, they are losing. No matter how much money they get, it will never be enough. You simply cannot win betting on bitches. You simply cannot win, and there is always a camera on you.

"Hey, man, you can just put that beer in the back of my truck," says a patron.

I hear this or a variation of this comment at least ten times a day. I stopped making any sort of response years ago. These men, along with their fathers and sons, mothers, wives, and daughters, are all hooked up to the same giant mechanical brain.

This brain hovers above the stratosphere in the big black sky and has nothing to do with God. It is man-made. From it hang billions of wires that are skinnier than rat hair. Most people (id est—the humanoids) cannot see these wires. But on a clear day, if I squint hard enough, I can see all the wires playing Dr. Tangle and entering the base of everyone's brains at the back of their necks. I cut mine long ago, and it was a painless procedure, seriously.

Nevertheless, I would like to think that I serve a worthwhile purpose at this racetrack. My beer will make some sad men happy, if only for the few fleeting moments of artificial happiness that a buzz provides. But in reality, the alcohol I supply to these patrons is not intended to make them happy so much as it is to impair their wagering sensibility. I help loosen their wallets by subtly drowning out their memory of how badly they suck.

When one of these sad men bets a twenty-dollar exacta on the two and five dogs, the mutuel clerk types it in the United Tote machine, which prints out a little ticket. If his bitches do not win (which will be the case), then this man just paid twenty dollars for a little white piece of paper, a two-minute scrap of hope. The money their own night-mare days afforded them is being spent on *nothing*. But everything makes perfect sense as long as I keep squinting.

"My truck's parked right out front, buddy."

Boss

Just how he looks is bad enough—a big, tall black guy with that big, Jheri-curled hair and those gay white dress shoes. But then he's gotta be talking crazy talk to himself, talking one minute about how he hates everybody and can't stand being around 'em and the next how he loves everybody and wants to save 'em all. He ain't right. Here he goes again.

"I am a child in my romanticism. I am a flipper baby in my idealism. And admittedly, I cannot look an adult in the eye without laughing. But all things considered, I am fortunate. Studies show that considering my personal back-ground, family history, and the habitat in which I grew up, I should be in jail or dead by now. Dead or in jail is the con-dition of most of my brothers, the normal ones of the fam-ily. I should be in jail or dead, but instead I get the beer to the dog-track patrons and look forward to my future. As I said, without contraries, there is no progression."

"You're really gonna have to stop talking to yourself like that," I says. "I've had reports of you scaring some cus-tomers. And by the way, I've been walking alongside you for ten minutes, you crackhead."

"Joe is a redneck. It says so on his truck," says Johnson. "But Joe does not have to advertise his social status on his vehicle. Even if he rode a moped and walked around with nothing but his Kentucky cap on, his position as pure white trash would be evident just from the empty look on his face, the same look that eighty-five percent of the people in this town possess. Roger that."

"Shut the fuck up, Johnson," I tell him. Shit, that boy pisses me off, but he's a hell of a worker—I'll give him that. And for some reason, there's something comforting about having him work for me. Plus, he's been here longer than me even—nearly ten years.

"Hey, man, you can just put that beer in the back of my truck," says a patron. I smile and laugh. I wouldn't mind getting that beer in the back of my own truck, to be perfectly honest.

"Joe, I am just trying to get through the nightmare day," says Johnson. "If I had someone to talk to, I would talk to them. For instance, let me talk to you, Joe. Let me ask you: Do you have any dreams?"

"No."

"I do. I want to rock it for the sake of goulash on the conch shell caviar table of life. I am playing for keeps, but not in the geometric sense of the word."

Johnson laughs at himself in that big, annoying laugh of his.

"Shit, boy. I sure would like to be on whatever you're on," I tell him.

"I hate it when people say things like that."

"Shit. Come on, boy. It's only fair that I'd think you was on drugs by the way you act."

"Hey, man, I'm parked right outside," says another patron. I just kind of laugh politely since I heard a similar joke a minute ago. Johnson shakes his head.

"I guess you would find it unfathomable if I told you that I have never done drugs in my lifetime," says Johnson.

"No, I couldn't fathom that. Not with how you are. And specially not after hearing your brothers are drug dealers."

Another customer spots the beer being pushed by.

"Hey, man, my truck—"

"Shut the fuck up!" yells Luster at the customer. "You people act as if you have never seen beer before! I appreciate your attempts at reaching out with humor. I really do. But you are not being original! You people are stale. You people are stale!"

"Johnson! Shut up!" I says. "I'm sorry, sir. He's on drugs."

Luster

Aurora, Ember, Opal, Ray, and I got dressed up tonight in formal evening wear (shirts untucked) and went roller skating all over the downtown streets. We are tired now, so we loiter on the sidewalk outside a local hangout, Rookies Sports Bar, occasionally making grotesque faces at the patrons inside.

I am so sick of my pointless job. I almost got fired again today. I think I will quit.

"You say that every day," says Ray. My effeminate Iraqi friend speaks the truth.

I know, but I mean it this time. It is time I crawl out of this life and start getting big. Statement: In order to do so, our rock band is going to have to start practicing more.

"It's not our fault," says Aurora. Despite her confinement to a wheelchair, she still wears roller skates. "The only time we get to practice is when your house is free." My beautiful Satanist friend speaks the truth.

We had our first band practice five months ago. Since then we have only had five practices because we have to work around my brothers' schedules. As long as only one brother is at my house, our practice can go on smoothly. But if there is more than one brother present, our power-pop new wave heavy metal punk rock music cannot compete with their animalism and ridicule. Besides the problem of my brothers, I also have to work around the schedules of my bandmates' "real world" obligations, those obligations to family, work, etcetera, etcetera, nut sack, nut sack, nut sack, nut sack.

To say the least, five practices in five months is not the proper amount of attention that my hopes and dreams deserve.

Maybe we could try playing at Opal's again.

"You saw how my old neighbors called the cops on us!" says Opal. My elderly rock and roll friend speaks the truth.

Ray lives in an apartment, so that is no good. What about your house, Aurora?

"I'm still fighting with my dad. He won't even let me have friends *over*, let alone have a band playing in his house."

"What about *my* house?" queries Ember.

"No, little skittle," says Opal. "We can't risk your parents finding out that I let you run around with all these guys. They just wouldn't get it, and I'd be liable to lose my gig babysitting you."

We will just have to continue practicing at my shack.

We will just have to build Rome.

"I can't wait 'til we play a show," says Aurora. "That's the only thing I miss about my old job, being on stage."

"I'd be missing giving the sailors lap dances, myself," says Opal.

I think that gradually my bandmates will come to associate this band of ours with the future good or the good future, the tomorrow that can drag us through today. They have just the right amount of discontent and individualistic life force to drive us upward, and more importantly, the humanoids in the "real world" are showing no signs of letting up on The Conspiracy of Mediocrity, the two-hundred-year plan that The Thoughtless Confederacy subjects us to daily. The humanoids don't know that it's every ounce of insincerity and ignorance that fuels the hope rockets we keep within our amplifiers and p.a. speakers, those ambitious mechanisms which can propel us out of dead end town.

IV. She's Got Spunk

Opal

They got us sitting in a big, happy circle like little kids in a kindergarten class. Some of us are in wheelchairs. Some of us are hooked up to machines. Some of us have grandchildren who haven't visited us in two years despite the checks we sent them.

But not me. And I'm not dressed pathetically like them either. When people get this old, it's almost like they give up on fashion altogether. Their outfits are so plain that I can't figure out whether I'm underdressed or overdressed.

The group therapist fag takes roll and doesn't mention the fact that one of us died since the last meeting. Then he pulls out some papers and says "take one and pass it over" like he always does.

"Okay, group. First off, this handout has a list of signs and symptoms of depression," he lisps. "Now, as I read them off, I'd like for you all to consider whether or not you've been experiencing them. Okay?"

"Lay 'em on me," I say. It's not like anyone else's keister was going to respond.

"Okay. Symptoms of depression: decrease of weight, increase of weight, loss of motivation, sleeping too much, sleeping not enough, uncontrollable crying, thoughts of suicide, becoming slower at everything, loss of concentration, loss of interest, and isolating yourself from everyone."

Just as I had reckoned, everyone in the world is depressed. The half-dead folks sitting in this circle are no exception. You can already smell the formaldehyde.

"So those are just some things you can be watching for to help you decide whether you're depressed or not, or to see just how depressed you truly are."

As it usually goes at these therapy sessions, there's complete silence. I don't know. Nobody really needs to say anything, I reckon, because the looks on their faces say it all. They've got shriveled dispositions and wrinkly brains and blank stares. And Kip's left with the task of filling in the blanks, but he's not too good at it.

"Wow. You all look like you're in really deep thought. Would any of you like to share with the group what you're thinking?"

Of course no one wants to share anything. I decide to say something just because I can't stand the silence.

"I'm thinking if this is gas in my stomach or what," I say.

"Hmm. Well, did this feeling start after you ate?" He always has a follow-up question.

"Don't worry about it, girlfriend. I'll make out. You asked what we were thinking, and I told you. Move on to someone else."

"Well, Opal, I don't think we should skirt the issue. Your gas problem might be a cause for concern because it might be a side effect of your medication."

"Honey, *trust me*. It's gas. I'm not on any medication." I just wonder exactly how many cocks this guy can fit in his mouth.

"Well, okay then. Whatever you say. Now, Trixie, the last time we met you said you had stopped taking your medication, and we talked about how it's important that all of you stick with the medicine that you've been pre-scribed. So have you started taking your pills again?"

"I can't," answers Trixie.

"Why not?"

"Because Jesus has been taking them."

"Okay. Like I told you last week, Trixie, you're going to have to confront Jesus. Jesus has to realize that your medication is for *you*."

"I know. I'll talk to him tonight."

Shouldn't we be laughing right now? That's a ques-tion that's always on my mind. Not laughing *at* her or *with* her, but *for* her, I guess. But the princess has already moved on.

"Now Blanche, how is *your* new medication working out?"

"What does it mean when it feels like my ears are on the bottom of my head?" Blanche replies.

I look around to see if anyone else is wanting to laugh. They're not.

"Well, I'm not sure," says Kip. "Do you think your new medication is causing you to feel like your ears are on the bottom of your head?"

"Yeah. I think so. Either 'cause of that or 'cause I'm a horrible person, and I'm going to hell."

"No, baby. You ain't goin to hell," says Trixie. "You just need to invite Jesus into your life. The only thing is, once he's there, you can't get him to leave."

I can't take it anymore. I let out a big laugh that had been building up as bad as the gas in my belly. Trixie laughs some too, along with a few others. It's about the only signs of life this group has shown in the three months since I've been going here.

"It's good to laugh," says Kip. That's the most helpful

piece of therapy he's ever given us, and he may have just had the breakthrough he's been hoping for.

Therapist

I remember from my college group therapy classes how important it is to maintain control of your group, so I try to steer things back on course. *I've* found the best way to get out of these sticky situations is to just change the subject!

"Now I think we better move on to Carl. Carl, last week you told us you wanted to die."

Carl is *sooo* grumpy! He refuses to smile!

"Yes. That's right, and thanks for bringing it up again in front of everyone."

Well, *excuse me* for doing my job! "Uh-huh. Now, do you still feel this way?"

"Yep. I still want to die. I'm tired of this life. In fact, I would like to die as soon as possible."

"Okay. Well, Carl, hearing you say that really saddens me, because I care about you, and so does the rest of the group. We don't want Carl to die, do we, group?

They just kind of mumble "no." They are no help. (*As usual!*)

"You said the same damn thing last week and the week before that," says Carl. "I just don't care anymore. I'm old and I'm tired and I'm sick of you telling me that I should live when I don't want to."

"Well…I want to help you." I really do.

"You people just don't understand. '*I want to help. Can I help you?*' No. If you really want to help, pray to God that

I die. Say, 'Lord, please kill Carl.'"

"Well, I'm just not going to do that, Carl." I think back to my favorite textbooks. "Hmm...Okay–scenario: What if you could have one wish–anything in the whole, wide world. What would it be?"

"To die before noon," he replies.

"Hey, it's 11:45," says Opal. "You better watch out, Carl!"

"Opal, please! Don't be so insensitive. Carl is hurting right now." She is *awful*! I wish she would go someplace else.

"That's okay," says Carl. "I don't mind. It *is* kind of funny."

"Well, I don't think it is. Carl, remind me before you leave to have you sign a suicide contract for me." He waves his hand dismissively at me. "Well, okay. Let's talk about you then, Opal. Have you made any lifestyle changes since we last met?"

"You mean have I quit gettin some derriere? No! At my age, what difference does it make?"

"Well, your nieces sent you here because they were worried that you were being a little promiscuous, and they thought that was a bit abnormal, and to be honest, I would have to agree."

"What's wrong with being abnormal?" she asks defensively. Okay, Kip. Stay in control. Keep it together.

"Well, nothing. I guess I shouldn't have used that word. Maybe I meant 'unhealthy.'"

"Lay off, Kip."

I might be mad if she hadn't called me by name.

"Well, let me ask you this: Why do you think you behave the way you do?"

"I could ask you the same thing."

Think fast, Kip.

"But I haven't been spending the night with strange men that I met in bars."

"That's not what I heard."

That old *bitch*! The whole group is laughing at me now, even Comatose Connie, as we at the nursing home like to call her. This is the most life the group has ever displayed.

"Okay. Very funny. You won this round. But you never answered my question. Why do you think you behave like you do?"

"I don't know. I guess 'cause I just have a tarlit load of wild oats to sow. Luster tells me I'm aging backwards."

"And Luster is the young African-American gentleman with whom you socialize?"

"Yeah. The black guy."

"Okay. Well, that's interesting. Why do you think you associate with someone so markedly outside your own social group?"

"'Cause I'm loony in my old age. Is that what you want to hear?"

"No. I want to hear the truth."

"*He wants to hear the truth,*" echoes Carl, mocking me. The group laughs. Urgh!

"Fine, Kip. Truthfully, I reckon I *am* loony. I guess you could say I always have been. Never bothered marrying a man. Never could start up a family. Never had the desire to be called 'mammaw.' I don't know. All I know is I'm eighty years old, and I don't want to die."

As Opal is talking, I notice that she has the entire group's undivided attention. I wonder if I should cut her off as she rambles on and on.

"And why not go wild in your twilight zone? Why

screw around, spring breakin when you're a stupid kid and you gotta live with yourself and your mistakes for sixty more years? My time is right now. I drink, I smoke, I get laid, and I'm alive, goddammit. If you got a problem with that, then you can just kiss my elderly white ass."

Poor thing. She probably doesn't even know what she's saying. After hearing her talk like that today, I'm afraid her nieces were right in wanting to put her in a nursing home.

"Okay. Well, that's nice, though I really wish you'd tone the language down. But let's move on to Gertie. Now, Gertie, you've been having trouble keeping your oxygen from getting disconnected. Why do you think that is?"

Opal

I don't know why we have to hang around at the public swimming pool, what with how so many people secretly piss in it. But there's nothing else to do in this poor excuse of a town, and at least Ray likes it here. Ember and I brought our basses since neither of us likes to swim, and I'm teaching her some Maiden. Meanwhile, Aurora's playing that game she likes with the guys.

"Are you more like fleece or leather?" she asks.

"Fleece," says Luster.

"Leather," says Ray.

"Are you more like pancakes or waffles?"

"Waffles," says Luster.

"Waffles," says Ray.

"Are you more like a bath or a shower?"

"A bath," says Luster.

"I just can't know. I just cannot answer that," says Ray.

I make Ember play "Innocent Exile" with me. She's really getting good. She has a crudload of potential.

"That's good!" I say. "You all, this girl gets better every day! I'll declare, she can play as dirty as Cliff Burton."

"Rock onward, rabid child," hollers Luster.

"I sure do hope we can go on tour or something with this band," I say. "I'm thinking by the way they've been talking, my nieces and that therapist boy are wanting to lock my rear up in a home."

"We won't let them," says Aurora.

I won't let 'em, either. I'm not gonna let 'em do anything with me, just as long as I can remember who I am.

While I was talking, Ember ran off to splash water on the tanning people, and now Aurora has resumed her game.

"Are you more like bacon or sausage?"

"Sausage. Definitely sausage," says Luster.

"Sausage," I agree.

Ray doesn't answer, though I'm fairly sure he would say bacon. He's mesmerized by some mustached fellow across the way who's rubbing on suntan lotion.

"Excuse 'ems," says Ray, and he prances off toward the man. I gotta give it to him. That Ray sure does have stick-to-it-iveness. With a spirit like that, one of these days, he's gonna find exactly the man he's been looking for. Course, that never did work for me.

"There he goes again." Aurora and I watch Ray do his thing. "So how are things going with you and the Ken's Fried Chicken guy?"

"Ooh! Great!" says Aurora cheerily. "I really think he

respects me. He's easy to work with, and he hasn't even asked me for a blow job."

"Maybe you've finally found a good one," I say.

"God, I hope so."

It's just so hard for unusual people like us to find anyone. I reckon that's one of the reasons why I finally got so I'd just take anybody, around the time I turned seventy-three.

We hear someone yell "faggot," and Ray comes scurrying back to us.

"No luck?" I ask.

"No. I was mistaken. I hate this. But at least I was able to block the punches he gave me."

"Cheer up, Ray Fuquay," says Luster. "You want to go for a dip? I know how that makes you feel well."

"Okay!"

Luster can't even swim, but he knows Ray doesn't like to get in the pool by himself. Luster can be a real good guy if he likes you, just like he can be a mean ol' sonbitch if he doesn't. He's got so much to offer people, if they'd just give him a chance, and if he'd just give *them* a chance. But it's pretty rare that both sides are willing.

As I'm proceeding to teach Ember some Dead Kennedys, Ray and Luster climb on up out of the pool. We're right in the middle of "Stealing People's Mail" when I hear Aurora gasp. I look up to see that Luster's shorts have fallen down.

In the station wagon on the way home, Luster won't speak to any of us.

"Luster, don't feel badly," says Ray. "You cheered me up majorly. You made me feel much more mannish about my manhood today."

"Shut up, gay-wad," replies Luster.

"Luster, I've known about your tiny wang for a couple of years," I say. "What's the big deal? I haven't treated you any differently, have I?"

He doesn't answer me, but I know him well enough to know how to get through to him.

"Luster, I'm surprised you don't see the poetry in this."

"What do you mean, woman?" he asks.

"Why, you're such an original, it's in your bones. You were born not to be like all those typicals."

At this, he smiles and laughs that great big wild laugh, forgetting his worry. I have to admit, I would've made a great mother. It is a shame I never could find a decent man in this world that liked me back.

V. Mecca Lecca High

Ray

As it goes so oftenly, my wife is cooking the kitchen when I get to my apartment after the work. She wears bunned-up hair, an apron, and makes the house smell foreign.

"Hey, honey. How was the work today?" asks she.

"Eh, shitty as usual."

Milkah, Aymon, and I sit down for the dinner. Every night we try to do this. Tonight I notice Aymon's strange clothings for the 1th time, I think. He wears a baseball jersey, but not to baseball in. He wears gold necklaces and backward baseball cap. He reminds me of the dressings of Luster's brothers.

My son is funky. I feel more normal now. If only my wife could loosen up and wear sweatpants once in a lifetime.

The utensils scrape and chink the plates, and that is all we have. I just must say. Something.

"So, Aymon, I heard you not in coming home last night at all. What time did you get in?"

"'Bout six a.m."

"What were you doing out so late?" Or should I say it "early"?

"I don't know."

I try so hard to father him, but he's never home any more. No blame on him for not wanting to be here. His mother and I constantly yell words. Mean ones. That's why I've been out with friends so much. Needing to get away from this place. At least I always get home way before the bedtime. But my son is only 16 and should not be out that late (or early), and I want to do some father-ing here.

"Were you sleeping with girls?"

"Come on, Dad."

"What were you doing? Can't you tell me?!"

My wife suddenly yells words in Arabic, and I don't want to hear it.

"No! Do not revert to the old language!" I command. "We agreed that in the new home, we would speak new home's language. Now, answer it, Aymon. What were you doing out until six a.m.?"

"I guess I was practicin rappin."

"What do you mean, 'rappin'?" voices Milkah.

"You know. Rappin'. Like: Thundercat, Thundercat, Thundercat, whoa. Kitty litter, Lion-O. Mecca lecca hi, mecca tiny ho. Futon, crouton, I don't know. By the power of Grayskunk he, climbed into the shit with me."

Oh my ass. I hear this rhythmic talking coming from my only child's lips, and I see the wife has a terrified look on her face. Just like mine. For once, my wife and I have on the same pagedness.

"Listen to him!" cries Milkah. "Look at him! Look at what this country has done to him—to us! Are you happy, Raykeem?!"

"Quiet!" I order. "Please, Aymon…who taught you how to do this stuff?"

"I learned it from my friends at school. We started our own rap group. We're called 'Mothah May I.'"

My wife covers her face. I guess alone I must do the

dealing with this.

"Son, I'm glad you found a place for music in your heart and life. I play band, too. But judging by what I just heard you did, I must now ask you something...I always hoped this day would never come. Son...have you been smoking marijuana cigarettes?"

Milkah uncovers her face. We stare at our son. Afraid of the answer.

"Uhh...I don't know. *Kind of?*"

My wife screams Arabically. I cover my ears to shield it. She pulls my hands off the ears.

"That is it! We are moving back to Iraq!" she says.

"Back, back, movin back to Iraq. Got my foot in a cast and a fanny pack," "raps" my son.

"It can't be so!" I mouth loudly. "We can't go back now!"

"Two loked-out G's playin *pin*ball, mad collectors of rare an*tique* dolls."

"We've lived here two years, Raykeem. Face this–you are not going to find that man!"

"Yes I will!"

"What are y'all talking 'bout?" questions Aymon. "Is Dad gay?"

"No!" says I. "I wish people would stop saying that!"

Not gay. I promise.

"I'll tell you what I talk about," says Milkah. "Do you want to know why we rearranged our lives and moved to America?"

"I thought it was for freedom."

"We lied to you," says my wife.

Wife

"We moved to this country because your father wants to apologize to an American soldier that he shot in the Gulf War."

I had never heard myself say it aloud before. It's even stupider sounding in the air than in the head. My husband is a foolish man with foolish ideas. I was a fool for giving up my life for him and following him here.

"*Why?*" my son asks.

"I just feel awful about it," says Raykeem. Fool! War is what men do! They shoot at each other. Men have always fought, since before men were men. They have always fought wars and always made love. Perfectly natural. Why should he *feel awful* about it? It is not as if it is something personal.

"Why didn't you tell me?" asks Aymon.

"I didn't want you to think I was a bad person for shooting someone," says Raykeem. That's not the only reason. He doesn't want his son to tell people that his father is totally nut-balls in the head.

"*I* didn't tell you because I didn't want you to think your father was fruitcake," I say.

"I already thought that. Look at how he dresses."

I look at his father. He is wearing the stringy tanktop and short shorts like he likes.

"This is how United States peoples dress!" says Raykeem.

Raykeem Fuquay is not gay. He looks and acts like so, sissy and lovey and so, but he is all man. I do wish he were into penis for an excuse to get out of all this.

"How do you know the guy you wounded lives here?" asks Aymon.

"I don't for surely, but he's gotta be located some-where down here nearby. I saw he was wearing a Kentucky Wildcats logo on his military helmet. We chose to settle in this town for now since there were so many of such logos seen here."

I look at my son looking at his father strangely.

"Look, I realize our reasons for moving here may seem somewhat, uh—"

"Retarded?" says Aymon.

"Yes. But who gives a care?! No regrets here!" contin-ues Raykeem. "I've grown to love this wacky country. I love the people. So diverse. Could I be friends with black men and little girls in Iraq?"

I can no longer take this man's shit. I jump up and throw my napkin on the table.

I run off to the bedroom before they can stop me. I don't care if we ever sit at the eating table again. I don't care if either of them follows me back. I want to go back where we belong. I don't care, even if I break this home for good.

Ray

We practice the band music in Luster's dirty living room. It is tiny here. Not a good place to be in general. We don't make it better, because I'm not for suresome, but I think our music is sucking badly.

Aurora got the beat but hits cymbals and floor-tom too oftenly. She's giving off a bad noise. Ember's four-string thing is too big for her, and she barely can stand up with it. Opal plays electric guitar awesomely, but she plays solos when she probably should not. I am having bad trouble remembering what I am playing on my keyboard guitar. But at least Luster is putting everything in the world into his singing.

"Girl, you move like a squirrel!" he sings. "I said gir-ir-ir-irl, you move like a squirrel! And I found the cure to the common cold. It's you!"

Then young Ember falls over with her big guitar on top of her. Luster tells us to stop playing.

"That sucked a possum's ass," he says. "That was crap quadrupled. I do not even know if that was rock music or not. Ray, did you even know what song we were playing?"

"'Hygene Bygene,' right?" I asks.

"No!" shouts Luster. "It was 'Squirrelly Girl!' Was that not obvious!?"

"I'm sorry. I have a lot on the mind." Like others, Luster gets very impatient sometimes. He seems obsessed with moving forward. While I am feeling so behind.

"Fine," he mouths. "Let us move on to 'Classroom Assroom.' You start that one, Ray."

"Right." I tell my fingers to play an opening melody, when I notice that Luster is giving me a dirty one.

"Hold on," he says. "That was not 'Classroom Assroom.' That was 'Ironic Decency.'"

"I'm—I'm sorry." To be honestly, I had no idea of what I was playing. It may very well have been Spin Doctors for everything I know.

"Is there something wrong, Ray Fuquay?" asks Luster.

"It's...it's just that my wife and I had the big fight last night. Now she's going to take my son and return to Iraq."

"Oh my God. Is she serious?" asks Aurora.

"Afraid so. She was packing up her 'jamas this morning."

"Bummer," says Luster. "No, let me update that. That is a flaming bummer."

They all tell me they are sorry. I don't know if it's the language or what. But it's hard to give up appropriate responses when people say they're sorry in sorry situations. Others have this problem. I said "I'm sorry" at a funeral once here. The woman said, "I am too." Words can't get it through sometimes, or all the times.

"Thank you. But okay, 'Classroom Assroom,' take two."

"Hey, you have had a rough day today, Ray," words Aurora. "Maybe we should call it a night."

"Perhaps so," voices Luster. "This practice is sucking Belinda Carlisle anyhow."

With the day problems getting in on the night's thunder. It seems like that is how our practices always end.

"We don't suck that bad for a band that's only practiced like five or six times," says Aurora, taking down the drums.

"Exactly. That is the problem," tongues Luster. "This was only our sixth practice. We should be practicing like six times a *week* if we really want to get somewhere."

"You know your brothers wouldn't go for that," says Opal.

We hear deep, booming car speakers that shake the whole house. Another form of night's thunder working against us. Boom, boom…boom.

"Speaking of my brothers, here they are," yells Luster over the noise. "Aurora, why not patch things up with your dad? Your house would be perfect for practice."

Luster is right. Aurora has a soundproof basement, and she lives in a rich neighborhood with not much neighboring. But as it goes so oftenly, a person is the problem. Since Aurora went Satanist, her dad will not speak to her.

"It's not that simple. He's convinced we're like a death metal band. I know he wouldn't allow it," says Aurora.

"Tell him we are not death metal. Tell him we are a power-pop new wave heavy metal punk rock band that rocks to the fifth power impossibly," speaks Luster.

The noise from outside stops, and three of Luster's brothers enter. They are big guys wearing sunglasses, basketball jerseys, bandanas, baggy jeans, gold jewelry, and all named Jerome.

"Ah, fuck. Y'all freaky mothah fuckas playin that freaky shit again?" words Jerome.

"Yes, Jerome, you assface. We call it rock music," says Luster.

Jerome throws a brown paper bag on the couch. I can tell just by looking at it that it's probobably bad. But I totally realize it might only be groceries. I don't care what Luster says. People still deserve the doubt benefit.

"Well, speaking of rock, little brother, Jerome and me finally got us a shitload of crack rock, ya know whum sayin, and we gonna sell that shit now, know whum sayin, so you and your mothah fuckin friends should fuck off, ya know whum sayin."

I could not speak worse. Jerome throws a big gun down on the coffee table. The other Jeromes stand on both sides of Aurora.

"Shit, Jerome," says Jerome. "We might let this one stay, ya know whum sayin. Whuzup."

"Hi," says Aurora. She looks very uncomfortable like.

"Whuzup," words Jerome.

"I guess congratulations are in order for my brothers," says Luster. "Selling crack is the pinnacle of their earthly careers. They have been waiting their whole lives to graduate from selling marijuana and acid to selling crack."

"Shit yeah, mothah fucka," replies Jerome.

"Why not reward yourself by watching *Scarface* for the thousandth time?" asks Luster.

"Probably will, you know whum sayin," replies Jerome.

I think I am the only one that notices that Ember has just taken a Ziploc bag full of whitish stuff out of Jerome's brownish bag. But this could still be groceries. She can easily hide the baggie underneath the big T-shirts like she wears.

I say nothing. Ember is a very bright bad girl. I'm sure she knows how she's doing. I don't want to get anyone in trouble. So I keep it quiet. I shut my mouthhole and let things be.

The brothers still stare at Aurora. She smiles nervous like. In public places, she always feels self-conscious. Thinks people are looking at her. But that is probably because they are. Right now is such.

"Uhh, Luster, maybe I *could* denounce Satan for the sake of the band," she says nervilously. "Besides, my dad *is* a minister. He's always preaching about forgiveness."

So does my heartless wife with her Allah, Allah, Allah.

VI. Raging Whore Moans

Aurora

Does anyone ever look at me and feel guilty for having legs that work? Do they count their blessings? Do they pity me? Or do they curse the fact that I'd make a lousy whore and that I'm a useless waste of ass?

I don't have to worry about that last question with David. He treats me like he'd treat anyone. I might as well not have the wheelchair. Of course, he has his flaws, but none of them are tragic. His hair reminds me of a Backstreet Boy, he likes jewelry too much, and he dresses way too plainly. Plus, I'm pretty sure he's one of those guys who went from liking country to rap between his sophomore and junior years and changed his wardrobe accordingly. But the superficial stuff doesn't matter anyway. Just so he's good to me.

"So I said, 'I'd tell you...but then I'd have to kill you!'" says David. Oh yeah. His sense of humor is way average, too. The Mexican guy he's talking to laughs at him anyway, though.

"All right. We'll keep in touch, bro," says David, doing what he calls networking. "You go help yourself to some chicken. Get one of the girls to pump you some beer."

"Thank you," says the Mexican guy. David turns to me.

"That reminds me—we should eat Mexican sometime. I know of a place that has phenomenal burritos."

"Yum," I say.

A guy eating a chicken leg runs into me. I guess he

didn't see me down here.

"Excuse me," I say.

"Whoa. Sorry. Didn't see you down there."

I'm at a party at David's apartment, or his "bachelor's pad" as he likes to call it. He has one of these parties about once a month for no reason and invites his workers and his old friends from high school. He has a really nice place, but half the party is always outside on the sidewalk where the smokers are.

A couple of the girls are trying to get to David, but I'm kind of in their way, so they have to maneuver around me.

"Oh, I'm just getting in everybody's way–the story of my life."

After hearing me say this, David doesn't offer me any sort of reassurance, which kind of pisses me off. I roll back toward the wall, out of the way.

"Great party," says one of the girls.

"Yeah. Kick *ass*," says another.

"Thanks, girls. All I have to say is party hard tonight, 'cause you're gonna have to work hard tomorrow. We're gonna be up to our asses in alligators once the new liquid chicken special starts. But, uh, work hard, play hard. Right, girls?"

"That's right."

"That's my girls. Now go eat some chicken."

The girls walk away, and David notices me over by myself against the wall. He suddenly pulls from his pants one of those cheap disposable cameras.

"Hey–look sexy!"

I offer him a seductive but playful glance, and he takes my picture.

"I'm just gonna come out and say it. You are looking phalange-licking-good tonight," he says.

"Thanks."

He already said that once to me tonight.

David normally wouldn't be so insincere and careless like that. This reinforces a theory I have about people. My theory goes like this—if you want to be with a real person and experience that person's essence, you must be alone with them. The eyes and ears of any additional persons subtract from his or her essence. If you go out to eat with two of your best friends, you will not be with two complete persons, and they won't behave as genuinely as they would if they were alone with you. If you are at a crowded party with a friend, you only get a fraction of his or her real self. Apply the same idea on a national, global, or even evolutionary scale, and everything that has ever happened might make better sense.

Boyfriend

To be honest, *everybody* is looking good tonight. I look around and see ass. Sweet ass. Sweet ass that I know for a fact to be sweet, if you catch my meaning.

"Hey, David, I've been meaning to talk to you about something," says Aurora. Oh, great. This better not be one of those talks like, Oh, I want to know where we are right now, and that sort of shit.

"Talk to me." Her boobs rule. Too bad she's in a wheelchair. Otherwise I'd be hitting it. I'd tear that up.

"Well, my band's trying to get on a more consistent practice schedule."

"Cool." Cool. No relationship bullshit.

"I know. So, we definitely want to practice Thursday

nights, and I was wondering–"

"Sure. You can have Thursdays off."

"Really?"

"Yeah. I'll give that shift to Candy."

"Oh–are you sure she won't mind?"

"Yeah. She owes me anyhow. It's cool."

"Thanks, David. You're the best boss I've ever had."

"Baby, don't think of me as your boss. I'm also your boyfriend."

"I know. Thanks for being so good to me. Most guys wouldn't even take a chance hiring a girl in a wheelchair."

Most girls in a wheelchair don't look that fucking hot. Besides, she's just the biscuit maker.

"Hey–you're still beautiful."

"Thanks."

I'm the man. Now is the perfect time to pop her the question. I've been waiting for this moment since I hired her sweet ass.

"Hey, while we're talking, there's something *I've* been meaning to ask *you* about."

"Is it about the popcorn chicken special? I swear–I thought biscuits were included and–"

"No. Forget about that. It's about this idea I have. How would you feel about posing for a calendar?"

"I don't think I'd like that, if it's the kind of calendar I think it is."

"Oh–no nudity, baby. I'm talking about bikinis, maybe lingerie, and maybe sort of holding your own titties kind of stuff. Tastefully done, of course."

"That's what they all say. That's something I may have done back when I was a stripper. But not anymore."

This is what I was afraid of. Time to turn on the ol' David charm. I act all bashful and shit.

"Um, well, um, what if you knew that *I* was the one making the calendar?"

"That wouldn't make any difference…Why would *you* be making a calendar?"

"It's for business. Here's the deal: the Girls of Ken's Fried Chicken Calendar. It's the ultimate chicken promo!"

"Have any of the other girls agreed to this?"

"Yeah. All of 'em. But I've been saving December just for you."

"But I'm in a wheelchair. That's not sexy."

"We can work around that, babe." I lean down close to her, look at her right in the eye, and whisper, "You still have a great chest. So will you do it?"

"Just forget it. I'm not interested."

Ungrateful bitch. This is, like, not cool. I can see that she's gonna need some convincing, so I call over a couple of her co-workers to lay on the peer pressure.

"What's up?" asks Christy.

"Girls, try talking some sense into Aurora. She doesn't want to be in the calendar."

"*Why not?*" ask both of my girls.

"I just think it's kind of degrading," yaps Aurora.

"Remember when we worked at the Busy Booty?" asks Kristie. "Now *that* was degrading."

"Yeah. It *was* degrading, and that's why I stopped working there," says Aurora. "But I guess I might as well still be there if I'm still just a piece of ass even at a freaking Ken's Fried Chicken."

"Honey, the Busy Booty wouldn't take you back now in that wheelchair."

"Thank you for reminding me, Christy."

"Look, I'm just giving you girls a chance to show off your bodies," I tell them. "I figured you would like that, judging by the way you dress, Aurora." She's wearing a sweet-ass dress that really shows off those useless legs of hers.

"You shouldn't judge people by the way they dress, duh."

"That's true…So will you pose for my calendar?"

"No! God, David, I thought you were different! I thought you respected me!"

"Aurora, I do respect you. I mean—I haven't even asked you for a blow job yet."

"I don't do that."

"Oh, come on, Aurora. You're a preacher's daughter."

"And an ex-stripper," adds Christy.

"And a Satanist," adds Kristie.

"Ex-Satanist. My dad blessed me last night. Anyhow, so sorry to disappoint you all. Am I the only woman on earth who finds the thought of having a dick in her mouth revolting?"

Kristie nods. Christy licks her lips and closes her eyes.

"Look, Aurora, I'm sorry, but like you said, most guys wouldn't have even hired you. You're doing well to make biscuits at my Ken's Fried Chicken. Now don't you want to continue working there?"

She looks up and sees me and the girls looking down at her. Then she gets up from her wheelchair and walks out the door.

"Stupid bitch. Not cool. *So* not cool!"

Aurora

I'm glad to leave my wheelchair behind forever with that sleaze and those girls, the sluts whose most ambitious hope and only chance for greatness is to someday sleep with the President. The wheelchair bit was good while it lasted but ultimately ineffective. It was like a morality joke that no one got, much like my stripping career.

I'll be the first to admit that I was a fool for dating David. Anyone can look at him and tell what he's all about, but I was trying to practice what I preach and be open-minded. I suppose Luster is right. You give people the benefit of the doubt, and they disappoint you every time.

"That's my house," I say to the cabbie.

"You live *there*?" he asks as he pulls up to the mansion, its gates emblazoned with wrought iron "B's" for "Buchanan."

"Yeah. Thanks for the ride." I pay the man and get out and notice that he's looking me up and down, at my slutty black dress, my leather jacket, and my prostitute-red lipstick.

"What?" I snap at the foreigner through his open window.

"Nothing."

Dropping me off here was probably the highlight of his week.

The first thing I hear upon entering the front door is the excited voice of Luster.

Why he would be in my home, I have no idea.

"I agree, Reverend! God *is* inside all of us!" Luster affirms. Holy crud. He's talking to my dad. "He or She or It reverberates in the power chords that hit the hammer, anvil, and stirrups. When I am rocking it like a man-child in love is when I am godlike. Rock music is my religion. I *believe* in rock music. Furthermore, I rock it impossibly. And Reverend, I believe in rock music to help me through the nightmare day, and someday rock music will lead me to my own private paradise."

I can't interrupt just yet. I *have* to listen to my father's response to this.

"Interesting," says Father, or "Reverend Buchanan" as he's known to the rest of the community. "That's certainly one way to look at things."

"It *is*," agrees Luster.

"But now, Luster, I hope in your quest for your own private paradise, you're not going to wind up choking on your own vomit like those rock stars tend to do."

"No, Reverend. I am not a rock and roll cliché. I thought you would have noticed that by now. What I mean is that I want my heaven to be here on land. After all, as Vladimir Nabokov wrote, 'The hereafter for all we know may be an eternal state of excruciating insanity.' So why not have heaven on dirt?"

"You talk too much! Can we go now?" begs another voice. Ember's here, too.

"Isn't she precious?" observes my father. "I think it's great that you all have found an outlet in music."

"Outlet, inlet, call it what you will, will you?" says Luster. "They say that no man is an island, but I am a peninsula."

It's so funny to hear Luster and my dad conversing, listening to the mingling of two parts of my life that had until now been kept separate. It's kind of like your favorite teacher having a drink with your uncle, or your therapist watching TV with your co-workers. I wish I could get everyone together, just to see what would happen.

It's also funny just to think of Luster talking to *any-one's* parent. Strangely, I've never heard him speak of his own parents. I'm pretty sure his older brothers practically raised him (or something to that effect), and that as the middle child of thirteen, he in turn helped take care of the younger six. But Luster is just one of those guys who you don't even think of as having parents. He couldn't have come from a typical carnal union of two other people. A guy like that must have spontaneously generated.

"And what's the name of your band?" asks Father.

"I do not know yet, but right now we are leaning toward Well Educated White Males."

"Good deal," says Father.

"Or the Fuxtables!" says Ember.

"The *what*?" asks my father, and there is my cue to enter the living room.

"Where are your wheels?!" Luster asks urgently.

"Screw 'em. I left them at David's. What are you two doing here?"

"We wanted to see if we could help smooth things over with you and your dad."

"Oh. That's not necessary. Dad and I had a nice long talk last night." This is how badly Luster wants this band to work out. He must have taken a bus from his end of town to this one in hopes of securing us a practice space. He even brought Ember and her irresistibly cute face.

"Yes. We talked everything out," says Father. "We blessed her and have welcomed her back. We've put those dark days behind us. No more Satan, right?"

"No more Satan," I agree. My Satanism was just a phase. All teenagers go through phases, but I like for mine to be momentous. Admittedly, I was pretty stupid.

"Dad, I'm sorry. I hope Luster didn't frighten you." I see Ember crawling out of the room, getting her knees all ashy like little kids do.

"Oh, we ended up having a great talk. Luster has to be the most well-read young man I've ever spoken to. Luster, you are welcome in my home *any* time."

Father doesn't know how Luster weighs all words. He loves making people mean what they say.

"In that case, good Reverend, I will be staying the night tonight."

Father

I must change the subject immediately. If only a new topic will come. Ahh, yes.

"So! Rory! You're walking again! Wasn't that crazy, Luster? A perfectly healthy young girl *choosing* to bear the burden of riding around in a wheelchair? Have you ever heard of such a thing?"

"Actually, it was Luster's idea."

"*Oh?*"

The young man nods. I should be resentful of him, I suppose, for leading the flesh of my flesh down such a crooked path. But I can't conceive what wild place this man's titillating thoughts come from, and I am interested in hearing his justifications. So I listen.

"Reverend, let us be frank. Your daughter is beautiful, and naturally there are many men out there who would like to make her their own personal whoopee cushion. When I met Aurora, she was tired and sick of being seen as a sexual object."

"Okay, Luster, that's enough," says Rory.

"No," I say. "I need to hear this. Go on, Luster." I notice the adorable little girl is no longer in our presence.

She must have grown tired of this grown-up intercourse. My new African-American friend continues.

"Aurora tried dealing with her sexuality in her own hysterical way, but then I suggested the wheelchair idea. I thought if Aurora made herself dead from the waist down, that would take sex out of the equation in regards to her dealings with people, because, after all, in traditional copulation—"

"Luster! He gets the idea!" interrupts Rory at the climax of the young man's explanation. It actually wasn't that ridiculous an idea.

"Why didn't you tell me that's the reason why you were riding around in a wheelchair, Rory?"

"I didn't think you'd understand. Besides, every time we talked, you just started yelling at me for being a Satanist."

"Right. My daughter the Satanist." I look downward and shake my head in disgust.

"I had nothing to do with that, Reverend," asserts the boy.

"Look—it was a creative way to rebel, okay?" says my daughter.

I must admit, perhaps this "creative rebellion" of Rory's makes a favorable alternative to the rebellion of her older sister. Stacy saw to it that she became impregnated. Then she dropped out of high school and moved in with an older man (who was *probably* not the father). Chad soon left her, and I then bought her a home in California where she failed as an actress, got her G.E.D., went to college, and became an atheist. However, she assures me that, though she's not religious, she's very spiritual.

"So I take it the wheelchair idea didn't work as well as expected."

"Not really," replies the boy. "We failed to consider blow jobs. That is why she also should have pretended to have lockjaw."

"Luster! Shut *up*!" demands Rory.

"Now be nice, Rory. Luster is our guest...So why aren't you in your wheelchair now?"

"I realized tonight that people are gonna judge me no matter what. My boyfriend showed me that I'm just, like, breasts and thighs to him, just like I am to everyone."

"Rory, don't say that!" I bawl. "You are so much more than breasts and thighs. You have a gorgeous soul, especially now since you retrieved it from the Prince of Darkness. However, do you think that maybe if you would wear some baggier clothes, perhaps some culottes, these guys wouldn't treat you like they do?"

"I like my clothes! Why should I have to rearrange my wardrobe for others?"

"You rode in a wheelchair because of others, didn't you? Rory, you're not being consistent."

"You are right, Reverend," says the articulate young man. "She is not being consistent, but her inconsistency is something you should love about her."

"What do you mean, good buddy?"

"Would you prefer she be consistent to the behavior expected of a girl who wears a dress like that?"

My daughter self-consciously tugs at her miniskirt, trying to cover up more of her thighs.

"Why, no," I answer.

"And would you prefer she be consistent to the stereotype of a stripper being a dumbslut?"

"No."

"And would you prefer your daughter to be consistent to the pattern that so many preachers' daughters before her have set, of rebelling against their dads by tossing their snatches around like pocket lint?"

"Of course I wouldn't."

I could do without such language, but he is my guest.

"Then let us praise the Lord that this girl has had the good sense to worship Satan and ride around in a wheelchair she did not need. Can I get an amen?"

I don't know if it's his voice or the words he's saying, but this irreverent young man could make anyone a believer. His positions and thoughts are unorthodox but sound. His word is strong. His convictions seem impenetrable. Despite his forceful manner, he has lubricated the difficulty between my daughter and me, and I find myself agreeing with him.

"Amen."

But right after I testify, I am jerked back into the necessary reality of my earthly mansion, as from the other room emanates the arousing sound of something valuable being broken.

"Ember?" yells the fruit of my loins.

Aurora

We all run to where the noise came from, to my father's den where he keeps all of his expensive religious art. We rush in and find Ember looking up at us bearing the mean but cute scowl that she usually displays. The floor around her is littered with white, brown, and flesh-colored pieces of clay.

"My Jesus statue!" screams my father. I want to laugh, but I realize that, sadly, this moment must be tragic for him. He loves his statues. Luster is already on the floor, trying to piece together the fallen icon.

"Ember, what happened?" I ask.

"I pushed it over as hard as I could, and it broke." No excuses. She just likes to destroy.

"But why would you do that?" I ask.

"I thought *you'd* like it," says Ember as she holds up her hand with her pinky and index finger, making a horn symbol.

"No, Ember. No more of that stuff. No more Satan. Forget all that. You should have never paid any attention to any of that. I was just talking."

God, we have to keep a closer eye on her.

Luster is having no luck putting the pieces of Jesus back together. Meanwhile, Father looks like he's gonna blow, and he finally does.

"Goddammit! That's the most expensive fucking Jesus statue I have!"

Ember laughs, but I don't want to anymore. Father goes down on his knees and holds big chunks of the statue to his chest as if he was embracing a dying soldier. Luster crouches on the floor with him.

"We will clean it up, good Reverend. No problems here," says Luster.

"No!" growls my father. "Leave! All of you, leave at once!"

"So may our band please practice here? I had been meaning to ask you that," says Luster.

"Never! Get out!"

Ember grins and giggles some more, and she looks somehow different. That's when I realize that this is the first time in the year I've known her that I've seen her smile. She has always looked so cute, I guess I never really noticed the actual feelings on her little face. She's always angry or pouting or brooding over something and sometimes even seems depressed.

As we're walking out the door, I want to pick Ember up and shake her and yell into her tiny ears, "Don't be like that! You're eight years old! You shouldn't have a care in the world! You should be happy!"

But then I realize that I can't preach, because someone could just as easily say the same things to me since I'm a teenager, that these are the best years of my life and all that crap. Still though, a depressed child has to be the saddest thing on earth.

I'd give anything to be a kid again, before zits, breasts, drugs, jobs, boyfriends, death, and those nagging thoughts that make you constantly question everything around you and inside you. I didn't know how good I had it as a kid, when my thoughts were to the point and pure and true, when I immediately accepted anyone I met and they accepted me, when the concept of what other people thought hadn't yet entered my mind.

So here's my epiphany for the day, one that should be taught in grade schools all across the world: When you're a kid, you're as close to perfect as you're ever gonna be.

VII. Grade School Riot

Ember

I got my hands in my shoes. I walk like a dog all over the classroom.

"Na-hoola-hoola-hoola. Na-hoola-hoola-hoo," I say, some sounds I like to make.

"Ember! Get over here, *now!*" says my mom. Her name is Kristen. She is a bitch. She is very pretty and almost thirty. I hate her.

"Mr. and Mrs. Blackwell, I appreciate your coming in today," says Ms. Watson. She's my lesbian teacher. I hate her too.

"That's fine," says Mom. "But we have to be out of here by 3:30. I have to take our dog to agility class."

"I won't take up much of your time. I just wanted to talk to you about Ember's conduct. I don't suppose Ember has been bringing home her conduct notices for you to sign. She never brings them back to me."

"No. Have you seen any conduct notices, Don?"

"Uh uh," says my idiot dad. He's also almost thirty and sucks.

"You haven't seen them because I burned them all up!" I yell. I know it's wrong, but I love fire. When I'm around matches or lighters, I just can't help myself.

Fire is so pretty. I like to think about the whole world on fire. I see the earth from outer space. Instead of water, the oceans are made of fire. I have dreams about that sometimes.

"Well, I figured you should know that her behavior is getting out of control," says my teacher. "And if it continues, we'll have no choice but to consider expulsion."

"Oh, geez, is she *that* bad?" asks Mom.

"Uh, yes, she is. We expect instances of bad behavior in any third-grade class, but it's the intensity and the ferocity of Ember's bad behavior that, frankly, sometimes scares the other students and me."

"What has she done that's so bad?" asks Dad. He's dickless.

"Let's see. I have a list here. She's thrown scissors at other students, sprayed Windex in other students' eyes, carved 'Slayer' into most of the desks, accused students of being homosexual, accused *me* of being homosexual, she regularly sniffs gluesticks, she's been caught chewing tobacco three times, she writes cryptic messages on the chalkboards such as 'nightmare day,' she's tried to incite riots in the cafeteria, she does this thing where she writes down what I say before I say it—the list goes on and on."

"Well, what do you want us to do about it?" says my mom all bitchy. "We know how bad she is. There's nothing we can do with her. We've tried everything. Ritalin doesn't work. Nothing works. She's just wild."

"Is she having any problems at home?" asks the dyke.

"Are you?" Dad asks me. I shake my head. Not me.

"She often talks about being friends with a stripper, an Iraqi, and a crazy black man. Do you know anything about that?"

"No," says Mom. "She lies all the time. The only person I know of that she hangs out with is her eighty-year-old babysitter."

"We think she might have imaginary friends," says Dad. Clueless bastards.

Mother

Was I ever as wild as my kid? I swear, if I had come as close to being an abortion as she did, I'd be trying to behave a little better. She's lucky I had already had one too many or she wouldn't even be here.

"Have you considered any psychological treatment?" asks the teacher.

"Look, Mrs…"

"Ms. Watson."

"Yeah, Ms. Watson," says Don. "Ember's never been a normal kid. She doesn't act like other kids act. Like when I was a kid, I got a kick out of simple stuff, like pushing the buttons in an elevator, you know whum sayin? But Ember could not care less about stuff like that."

That's right, Don. You *better* not tell anyone that our daughter has been to a therapist. We took Ember to a therapist for the first time when she was six because we noticed she kept rooting for the coyote and yelling "Die!" at the roadrunner. The therapist couldn't do anything with her.

She's just too much. Screw Don for getting me pregnant. I'd probably go ahead and go for a divorce if I weren't able to have fun on the side like I have been lately. And thank God for Opal always being able to keep Ember. Don and I like to have some us-time now that our daughter is getting to an age where she doesn't really need her parents. Besides, she seems to like Opal better than us anyway.

"Ouch! Dammit, Ember!"

Ember just threw a pair of scissors at Don's head.

"Ember! Get over here, *now*!" I order.

Now she throws crayons at me and Don.

"Go get her," I say to my husband. He obeys, and I resume this little conference with the teacher.

"She's such a cute little girl, Mrs. . ."

"It's Ms. Watson."

"Right. She's just so adorable on the outside, and it's hard to believe she's such a *monster* on the inside."

I hear three good spanks behind me, which usually shuts her up for a few minutes.

"That ain't cool," says my daughter after the last spank.

"Uhh—she's also extremely intelligent," says the teacher.

That's news. She never seemed all that smart to me.

"But I'll warn you. Should her behavior not improve, not only could she face expulsion, but also the school might contact social services, as Ember would perhaps best belong at the East Home."

"*The East Home for Girls?*"

"Yes."

"You hear that, Don? They might send our girl off to the East Home."

"Oh, *great*," says Don as he sets Ember in a desk.

They *cannot* send any daughter of mine to that skanky place. I used to hang out with some of the trash that lived there. God, I could use a big fat blunt right about now.

"What's the East Home?" asks my daughter.

"Don't worry, Ember. We're going to straighten things out," says the lesbian.

"I'll tell you what it is," I say. "It's a home where they send all the bad little girls, and most of them are really mean orphans."

"Ember, I know that you're really a good girl, and I

don't want you to have to leave this school *or* your home," says the teacher.

"She's not going to any home for delinquents," I say. "We're gonna change, Ember. We're gonna make you a good girl, aren't we?"

She gives me the dirtiest look and says, "You're not the boss of me, and someday I'm gonna grow up and fart all over you."

Ember

Mom said that after all the problems I was causing, she needed a vacation from her worries. The day after the conference with Ms. Watson, she and Dad left. They are in Cancun. They will be there for about a month. They left me at home with my babysitter. They took the dog with them.

I don't mind since my babysitter is Opal. Now Opal will be living in my house for the next month. Mom told her that she couldn't deal with things and needed to get away. She told her to make sure I go to school and stuff.

I live in a big, nice house in the suburbs. Now there are no adults in it. (Opal doesn't count.) We are finally free to do what we want. Opal and I started talking about our new freedom. Then she called the rest of the band.

Opal and Aurora move the couch against the wall. Ray jumps. Luster looks all around my big living room.

"Righteous," he says. "This is all ours for a month. The possibilities."

I help Luster and Ray bring the music stuff into the

house. Luster is so happy. He loves music so much. I love playing it, too. Now we can play it every day.

We get the stuff out of the station wagon. The neighborhood walkers and joggers look at us funny. I hate them.

Ray waves at them. He doesn't ever act tough. He is gentle and not like men.

People sometimes don't like to see all of us together. They would hate to see us as a band. They'd hate to hear us come together. That's why I love playing music with them so much.

Ray keeps waving. They look the other way. Why should I be a good little girl when the neighbors won't even wave?

VIII. Hey Suburbia

Cop

After we get the third call about some suspicious activity in the Hills, I get going. They say some suspicious-lookin guys (a black and a foreigner) are lurking around at the Blackwell residence. One of the ladies that called said that the family left for Cancun this morning, so something is probably up.

Just as I'm getting out of the car, I hear someone say "One, two, foot, shoe," and then some rock music starts. They ain't ten seconds into the song before I'm ringing the doorbell and pounding on the door.

An old lady wearing blue jeans and a shirt that says "Screeching Weasel" on it finally answers the door.

"What do you want?" she asks.

"Ma'am, that music's too loud. You can't be playing music that loud in the middle of the suburbs like that."

"But we just started playing ten seconds ago! We were just ten seconds into 'Awesome Possum.' Nobody could have complained yet."

"Well, they were going to. Do you mind if I come in, ma'am?"

She walks away pissed off and leaves the door open for me. I walk in and see a portrait of a good-lookin couple hanging in the foyer. I thought the name Blackwell sounded familiar. He's a lawyer I see at the courthouse from time to time. I actually think I may have arrested the wife once for meth.

I follow the old lady into the living room and see where the noise was coming from, and now that I seen it, I seen it all. There's a curly-haired black guy standing at a microphone, an Arab-lookin guy with one of them keyboard guitars, a little girl with a great big guitar, and a slutty girl behind the drum kit.

The old lady says, "Well, what do you want? You wanna watch us or something?"

"No, ma'am." The foreigner looks kinda scared and afraid to move. The black guy is staring me down. He looks kinda familiar.

"The eternal question," the black guy says into his microphone. "Is there a problem, Officer?"

"Well, no problem, but I'm sure someone was gonna complain about that noise. Listen—who's the head of this household?"

"I reckon you could say I am," says the old lady.

"This is your house, then?"

"Naw. The owners left for Cancun. I'm babysitting their girl, the bass player."

I look at the little girl. She's cute as hell, but she's giving me a real dirty look. Then she sticks out her tongue and strums her big guitar like she's mad at me.

"So you're the babysitter, and you're babysitting the kid. And who are these *other* people?"

"Our friends," says the old lady. "Why do you ask?"

"No reason. We got some reports of some suspicious activity at this residence. I just wanted to check things out."

"You don't see anything suspicious here, do you, Officer?" asks that hot young thing.

"Well, uh, I guess not, ma'am." I still gotta make sure

there's nothing going on here. "Hey, little girl, do your parents know you're playing that rock with these grown-ups?"

The little girl don't even answer me. She just stares at me. Meanwhile, the foreign dude looks like he's about to have a nervous breakdown, fidgeting and sweating and shit.

"Policeman, please! We break no laws here!" he yells in a shaky voice. "But okay! I'll confess it! Coming in America I was not familiar with urban traffic laws. I jay-walk! I jaywalk many, many time! I'm sorry! I—"

"Hey—take it easy there, chief," I say. "No one is in any trouble." Yet.

"Then will you *leave*?" snaps that hot piece of ass.

"Yeah, I'll leave. Y'all sure are a curiosity, though. I'll tell you that much."

I figure I must have pissed off the black guy by saying that, 'cause he's about to stare a hole right through me. I stare at him right back, and then I realize where I know him from. He's one of the Johnson boys, some of the biggest dealers in town. I've seen this guy before when I'd make an arrest at his shack. He'd be off on his own writing in his bedroom while his brothers were getting busted.

"Aren't you one of the Johnson boys?" I ask him.

"Yes. I am sure you are familiar with their work. But do not consider me one of them."

"Is it *Jerome*?"

"No. Luster."

"Well, Luster, you're a good ways from home, ain't ya?"

"Yes. I am breaking the social law, Officer, and so are the rest of my bandmates. If there is a problem with that, you can kiss my ass, figure of speech style."

"Watch it, mother fucker. I've put away plenty of your brothers, and I could just as easily do the same to you. As far as I'm concerned, you're guilty just for being related to 'em."

The boy shakes his head and just starts laughing like a crazy man. The whole time he's staring at me. He's fixin to say something when the old lady interrupts.

"You remember the way out, don't you?"

"Yes, ma'am. I'll be on my way. Just keep the noise down."

My work is done here, so I check out the slut again and look at the black boy one more time to show him who's boss, and then I head on out. Just as I'm fixin to leave, the black boy yells at me on his microphone.

"Oh, sweet lord, Officer! It just dawned on me like a black hole sun that there is something I have been meaning to ask a man in uniform!"

I turn around and re-enter.

"Okay, but you don't need no microphone to ask it."

He steps away from the mike and says:

"I have always wondered about a situation. I am sure that it is one that happens every day somewhere in the world, even in a small town like this one."

"I'm listenin."

"Let us say there is an individual driving his car down a lonely road at night, doing his own thing, minding his own business, obeying traffic laws, and keeping his speed at the posted limit."

"No problems there," I say.

"I guess not," says the gangster. "But then let us say that a second car comes up behind him and keeps getting closer and closer yet shows no interest in passing. Remember, it is night, so our individual can only see headlights creeping up behind his ass. When he sees that he is being tailgated, he speeds up."

"Right. What's your question?"

"So the second car keeps right on the tail of our individual, forcing him to keep increasing his speed, until finally he is driving well past the speed limit. At that point, the second car, the one that is doing the tailgating, turns on its sirens and patriotically displays its red, white, and blue lights. We know the rest. Pull over, please, license and registration, please, step out of the vehicle, please, here's your ticket, and so forth and so on. So my question to you is, who should be blamed here?

I ain't stupid. He expects me to say the police officer wasn't doing anything wrong, since after all, I *am* a cop. I know how to handle this.

"First of all, that wouldn't happen. Second of all, *both* of them are at fault. The cop should've had something better to do than follow around that driver. But the driver didn't *have* to speed up, though. Nobody was forcing him to. He didn't have a gun to his head."

"Would you say that the cop actually created this crime?" he asks. "It would have never occurred if he had not appeared."

"Now you're getting into chicken or the egg stuff, there. I gotta get going."

"Fry the chicken and scramble the egg. That is what I always say. But I am surprised at you. You said both drivers were at fault. How could the police officer be at fault, for as soon as the first driver exceeded the speed limit, the police officer was merely doing his job in pulling him over?"

That's true. Now he's making sense.

"That's true. Now you're making sense."

"Yes, sir," says the boy. "The police officer was just doing his job, being a fucking asshole. You push us into things like that and then wonder why we are the way we are. You push us out just so you can get things the way they are in your head, and then you do not even give us a chance, and none of you have guns to your heads, either."

Listen to all that bullshit. Sounds just like his brothers, like he's on crack.

"Shut the fuck up, Johnson. I'll be keeping an eye on you."

I hurry out so I can have the last word.

"And keep that noise down!"

Luster

The only thing I have in common with my brothers is a hard-core Jedi hatred for cops. My brothers hate cops because they interfere with their drug dealing. I hate them because they interfere with my life progress since they are the muscles of The Thoughtless Confederacy. We both refer to cops as "The Man," but I put much more weight in that term than my Neanderthal brothers do.

As we move our band equipment to the basement of Ember's house, taking our music subterranean so as not to disturb suburbia, I think about how my brothers' drugs are floating around in the fine homes above. In fact, my brothers' marijuana, acid, ecstasy, and now crack helped build some of these fine homes. The prominent business-men, lawyers, doctors, and real estate agents who occupy these homes not only ingest the drugs themselves but also get these drugs into town in the first place and then profit by selling to dealers like my brothers who go on to sell the stuff to everyone from blacks to whites to foreigners to politicians to the elderly to the unborn to pregnant teenagers to high school principals to playground children to PE teachers to college kids to housewives to meter maids to the poor to the rich to the middle-class to the tired, poor, and huddled, to the Jewish carpenters, the preps, the rednecks, the fags, the hippies, the bold and the beautiful, the shy and the repulsive, widows, orphans, amputees, introverts, extroverts, and all of their mothers, fathers, guidance counselors, mistresses, therapists, and former best friends. The one common strain in the wires attached to their brains is my brothers' drugs, those chemicals which temporarily make this world more tolerable.

Those prominent upper-class good guys with their cool out-of-state underground connections introduce the drugs to our town and sell them to guys like my brothers even though they would never give my brothers the time of year, or sit at the same burgoo table with them, or let their daughters date a man named Jerome. But money is being made, and everybody is cool with it. Cool, cool, cool. Everyone feels the same when they're making fabulous moolah and putting weird shit in their bodies. They all feel cool, and that's the way the giant mechanical brain likes it.

I have nothing against drugs. It's just the cool I have a problem with.

Our band has now safely evacuated to the basement.

We have a gnarly practice, so rocktageous that it comes across as subversive, almost anarchic. We rock harder than a peanut butter famine. I think after this practice I can honestly say that we are the best power-pop new wave heavy metal punk rock band that this town has ever produced.

"When are we gonna play in front of people?" inquires Aurora.

Soon, for time is our greatest enemy in this retrograde existence. I will be working on setting up a show. But for now, I better get back to the rut I call home.

"Don't go! Stay the night!" Ember pleads.

"Yeah. Y'all can just start sleeping over here if you want," agrees Opal. "I'm sure Ember's parents wouldn't mind, and who cares if they do?"

We all immediately accept the invitation since our home lives are so lonely and undesirable. I would take any chance to get away from my crackhouse home and the subhumans that live there. Ray's family has returned to Iraq, leaving him singular. Aurora's dad is still pissed about his Jesus statue and has really been on her case.

We move in and become the family that none of us ever had, the family that no one has ever had, if only for the few weeks that Ember's horrible parents have allowed us.

IX. Lonely Aliens

Opal

It's pretty late when we're done rockin out, but of course, Ember isn't ready to go to bed yet. So the five of us make fun of the TV for a while, crackin on the idiots on *The Real World*, the morons on *Blind Date*, and the assholes on E!'s *Wild On*. We also watch Jay Leno for a while just to see how awkward his interviewing will be.

Around two a.m., after making fun of *Roadhouse* on TBS, Ember makes us play Good Morning, Judge. How the game works is that one person sits in a chair facing opposite everyone else so he can't see what's going on. Then, one of the other persons goes up behind him and says, "Good morning, Judge" three times, only you disguise your voice by talking all funny. The person in the chair has to guess who said "Good morning, Judge."

The problem with us, though, is that each of us has such a unique voice and can't fake it. So it's impossible for the person in the chair to guess wrong.

"This game blows it," says Ray. "No one has guessed it incorrectish all night."

"I agree with Fuquay," I say. "It's bedtime for this booty."

"No!" hollers Ember.

"Yes!" I holler back. "We cannot play Good Morning, Judge all night, honey."

"I'm not sleepy!" she whines.

"Well, baby, I'm sorry, but we are. I know. What if I told you a bedtime story?"

She reluctantly agrees. We all get ready for bed and get situated in Ember's big, messy bedroom. Luster, Ray, and Aurora lie in sleeping bags on the floor with all the clutter, and I'm in bed next to Ember.

"What story do you want to hear?" I ask her. "I know 'Jack and the Beanstalk' and the first two seasons of *Magnum P. I.*"

"Tell me about the night that you and Luster met."

"You're too young to hear that!" says Aurora.

"Tell it!" screams Ember.

"Tell it!" screams Luster.

I had told Ember this story once before, and she got a kick out of it, so I'll tell it again if it'll make her angry little tush happy.

"It all started one Thursday night a couple years ago when I was—well, I was *playing* with one of my boyfriends. This was back when I just dated people closer to my own age, and this boyfriend died while we were in the act of…playing."

"You mean you were doing it," interrupts Ember.

"Right. So my date died, but the night was still young. I had the ambulance give my tail a ride to Gloria's, my favorite bar. The driver said he was sorry they couldn't save him and all that, and I told him to forget it, that it happens all the time.

"So I walked in the bar, and it's karaoke night, a night I normally avoid. Sean the bartender gave me my usual, which at that time was a Fin du Monde. (They special ordered it for me.) So I was sitting at the bar like I usually did, kind of feeling down after having my playmate croak on me.

"Just when I was starting to feel old again, I heard this gigantic voice scream over the opening chords of 'Some Guys Have All the Luck' by Hot Rod, or Rodzilla as I call him. The voice was screaming, 'I do not even need that smart-ass teleprompter!' I turned around from the bar, and that was the first time I saw Luster.

"He was lookin handsome in his flea market T-shirt, the one that says 'Hey now!' So then he started singing the opening lines. What were they, Luster?"

"Alone in a crowd in a bus after work and I'm dreaming," says Luster, already half-asleep on the floor.

"That's it. So he started singing, and his voice was so strong, and he was really gettin into it. He was a showboat even back then in front of a couple dozen skanks at a karaoke bar. He would rub himself all over all sexual and what have you, and he would kind of hop around, and lo and behold, he really *didn't* need that teleprompter.

"So I said to Sean, 'Who's *that* youngblood?' and Sean said, 'That's Luster Johnson. He's a regular here on Thursday nights. Kind of a weirdo.'

"And I said, 'Yeah, but he's a *hot* weirdo,' and then I got up close to the little stage, and I yelled, 'Hey! Show us your tits!' and I think it bothered him. He kept on singing and didn't show me his tits. But I wasn't through with his tuchis yet.

"A little later when he was at the bar downing some milk, I went up to him and said, 'Hey, biggun.' That's what I used to call him, 'biggun.' I said, 'Hey, biggun. You kicked rump up there tonight,' and he said, 'Thanks be to you.'

"I told him he was really playing for keeps, and then he gave me some of that old Luster talk. He said, 'Keeps?

Keeper Sutherland. Trapper Keeper. I always play for keeps' (or something like that). Then he explained how his karaoke singing was just practice for when he had a rock band one day that would conquer the whole world.

"I told him he didn't have to tell *me* about rockin out, 'cause I knew all about it. I lived for rock. Then I offered to buy him a drink.

"Well, he didn't want me to buy him a drink. He snapped at me and told me to go away, and he said he was liable to bite me just for having fallopian tubes. (Those are some female parts.)

"So I told him I'd take my chances and that my name was Opal Oglesby. Then he noticed my Dead Milkmen T-shirt. He said, 'I like your shirt, but within it dwells a humanoid of the worst design—woman'. I told him, 'Boy, you're about as fun as shopping for school supplies.'

"It turns out he was all pissy because this girl named Tonsillectomy Tina had stood his crupper up that night. He said he guessed she just didn't take their plans as seriously as he did, and that he guessed you can't go around acting like an alien without people treating you like one.

"I said, 'I think aliens are sexy,' and he could tell right then and there that I was just as big of a strange-butt as he was. I told him I was sorry about his getting stood up, and that I'd had a lousy night, too.

"He said, 'Nothing feels worse than being stood up,' and I said, 'Yeah, that's bad, but what about havin your date die on you while you're bonin?'

"He said, 'You win,' and then he let me buy him a drink after all. So that was the beginning. After that, we ended up dating for almost a year."

I check down on the floor. Luster is sound asleep, already drooling.

"And then I dumped his cheeks. The end."

Ember is still awake, but she allows me to turn out the light, only if I'll stay in the bed with her. I think how you gotta be careful nowadays with things like this just because some sickos have ruined it for everyone else. Anyhow, she'd never admit it, but I think Ember is scared of the dark, so I agree to stay in bed with her. It's more than her grandmas would ever do for her. Her grandmas are in their late forties/early fifties and are bigger sluts than I am.

After I take Ember to school the next morning, I have to go in for another fucking group therapy session. I promised my nieces that I'd go to the stupid things because they're the only relatives I've got. All the others are dead.

I'm kinda looking forward to today's session 'cause I'd like to see how Carl's doing. We slept together one day last week.

He comes in smiling for a change. I'm guessing he's not hoping he'll die now, thanks to my sexual healing. Beats the hell out of getting enemas all day, I'll tell you that much. He winks at me, but we don't let on like we've been banging each other.

Kip the faggot skips in and begins the session. He takes roll and doesn't mention the fact that one of us has had a stroke since the last meeting. Then he pulls out some papers and says "take one and pass it over" like he always does.

"Okay, group. First off, this handout has a list of ways you can improve your time management skills," he lisps. "So you can take those home and read them over yourselves. Okay. So now what I'd like to do is have what I call a 'happiness exercise.' I want you to think back to a time when you were *completely* happy. For instance, for me, my happy memory is when I cashed my high school graduation checks and went on a shopping spree at my favorite antique mall."

I'm sure Kip means well like everybody, but I just don't care for him. The guy makes no effort to get outside the picture we already have of him. We all know him just by looking at him or hearing his voice, and I think there oughtta be more to somebody than that, dammit. I think he just caught me rolling my eyes at him.

"So, Opal, would you like to start the group off and tell us a happy memory?"

"Shit. What the hell," I say. Better than listening to him talk about his antiques and his shoes. "The first thing that comes to mind is this thing I used to do with my ex-boyfriend Manny. This was about a month ago. I'd have Manny wear the same pair of underwear for two weeks straight, right?"

"Uh-huh," says Kip.

"And then, when the two weeks were up, I'd have him take off his drawers and hide 'em real good somewhere in my house. Then—now this is the happiness part—then, I'd sniff around my house all day until I found 'em."

I get a big laugh out of the group for that one. But Kip looks uncomfortable, acting like a prude even though he'll probably go home tonight and do the same thing with his Hispanic boyfriend. He looks at me like he either feels sorry for me or wants to hit me. Or I guess he'd be more likely to bitch-slap me.

"Oh, Opal. Oh." He jots something down on his little notepad. I know he's gonna tell my underwear story to my nieces, and they'll all be rarin to put me in a home once and for all to end my foolishness. But I've got a news bulletin for them: The foolishness is just beginning. The band's gonna practice every night at Ember's, and we're taking off soon whether they like it or not.

"Let's move on to Trixie," Kip continues. "And maybe we should just forget about the happiness thing. Just tell me what's been going on in your life."

"Well, I had a talk with my friend about him taking my medication like you told me to," says Trixie.

"Oh good. With Jesus, you mean?"

"Yes. And when I was talking to him, I got to thinking about some of the things Opal said, and well, long story short, we ended up sleeping with one another."

I give Trixie a big thumbs up. The rest of the group applauds her. Kip looks like he's gonna cry, or do something, I don't know what. I'm suddenly glad I've been coming to these things, just to show these old people that they don't have to be what they're supposed to. I wish Kip could pick up on that, but he's always too busy changing the subject.

"Okay. Maybe we should move on to Carl. Carl, you seem much happier this week. Why is that?"

X. Talk to Strangers

Ray

I can't get it understood. I once left my family to go to war. Now they have left me when I went for peace. Missing Aymon and Milkah, this last week has been better for my head. Since it's like familiness in the home here at Ember's.

Luster and I get home from the work near the same times. Aurora and Opal stay at home except for Opal taking and picking Ember up from school. Sometimes the females have dance routines to *Footloose* soundtrack figured out for us when we come in.

Once we have togetherness, we eat dinner. Every night. Sometimes going out to a place like Ponderosa. But usually ordering pizza or eating Opal's cook-out food. We listen to good music as we eat food and then when we digest it. We like records of those such as Swingin Utters, Pixies, Big Audio Dynamite, Vindictives, Billy Ocean, Boris the Sprinkler, and Go-Go's when we eat. We like Pogues, Trash Brats, Crash Test Dummies, Mullets, Andrew W.K., Cars, and Rezillos as we digest. Then we are prepared to rock out for the hours of night.

We enjoy not putting our equipment up. Then we make fun of the people on television or play something. We like the board game Guess Who? You have to figure out what person the other player has on a card by asking, "Does your person have blonde hairs?" or "Does your person wear a hat?" or such.

But Aurora changed the rules. When we play, you can't ask anything about how the way the person looks. Instead, you ask about the person's life. Like "Did your person date a baseball player in high school?" or "Does your person cheat on his or her spouse?" It is much more fun to play it this way. But also much harder. Luster plays the best. "Is your person Bernard?" "Yes!" "He's a pedophile!"

We go to bed when we are sleepy, crawling into sleeping bags on a childhood floor. Ember the little one needs a story to sleep to every night. Tonight I want to tell her it. I miss fathering. My own son so far away in Iraq.

Ember doesn't want to hear my stories of magic sitars and vagabond trickster tales, seahorses coming of age. She doesn't like fake stories for liking real ones. So I tell her about the way I met her.

"We met in kung fu class. It was my 1th night there. You had kung fued there many times before. The class was all ages and skills. Mainly children. I felt out of place in life as usual. But you sat next to my body and didn't laugh at me like others.

"I was there to learn to defend my body. I was tired of my body getting the whoop from the men whoms thought I was checking them out when I tried to figure out if I shot them in war.

"Pat was the teacher's name. He used his kung fu to get free Cokes out of soft-drink machines. That 1th night he chose you and me out when it was time to spar. He warned me that you could be dangerous. I told him I learned no moves yet and didn't want to fight a small girl. I didn't understand.

"I still didn't understand when he yelled 'fight.' You kicked me in my crotch. It hurt painfully, you kicked it some more. I fell down to the mat, you kicked it some more. You kicked me all over as I hurt on the floor. It was the biggest beat-up I had received up to that point. And kept getting worse! The other students yelled such as 'Yeah!' and 'Woo!' People love 'Woo!' in this country.

"Meantime, you yelled things such as 'Burn you up!' and 'Die!' I was scared and didn't understand while this child kept kicking my area. The teacher told me I was doing good because I blocked my privates, the focus of your attack. But then after he said that, you tried pulling my hands away from it, and the teacher said that wasn't right.

"You gave him the bad finger and proceeded kicking on my face and stomach. By this time, the crowd hush-hushed. The teacher tried pulling you off but had trouble. You yelled things such as 'I hate you!' and 'Kill 'em all!'

"The instructor finally got you off me. I was bruises and blood. You told me later you were taking kung fu because you wanted to learn how to hurt people better. You learned a lot on me that night, I think.

"After the class and my wounds dressed up, I left. I saw you in the parking lot, sitting on the curb alone. I felt the need to talk to you. I talk to persons because this life is too small not to.

"I said, 'I just wanted to say you kick good.'

"You said, 'Tell me something I don't know.'

"I didn't know what you meant and still don't. I didn't understand, and you told me to shut it.

"I asked you what you did sitting out there, and you said your mom was to pick you up. But she forgot to sometimes. This was such one of these times. I offered you a ride home. That was when I drove a taxi and always gave people rides.

"You told me that your babysitter Opal told you not to accept rides from strangers. But you said I was okay since you could already know you could kick my ass.

"In the taxi, you asked—and I'll never forget this—you asked why foreigners always drove taxis. I didn't understand then but do now. I had never heard such until then. That was the beginning.

"I gave you rides every week from then. Sometime shortly later you introduced me to Opal. She then introduced me to Luster. He inspirated me to not drive taxis so not to be predicted. I then worked at a tanning salon instead.

"But you and the others got me wrong saying I liked pee-pees. You used to always make fun of me, saying I liked men's butts and pee-pees. You all looked at me differently when I told you about not liking penis and the apology I needed to give to my man. The end."

Ember sleeps it up.

The next day is my day off from the tanning salon. But I don't get to sleep late like I like because Luster wakes me. He wakes everybody up every day samely. He says, "Get up! Time to face the nightmare day. A lot of assholes depend on you."

I let Luster talk me into going to his work with him. He's always wanting one of us to go with him. He hates work so much. And thinks having one of us there will make it better. He also hates riding on the bus. Like a little kid.

So I drive us in my Windstar to the dog racetrack. A place which I don't understand. Luster takes me back deep in the commissary to a little office with pictures of cars, half-naked women, and cars with half-naked women standing next to them. A middle-aged mustached man and two teenage boys trying to grow mustaches sit in the office smoking cigarettes.

"Good morning, jerk-wads. I decided to bring a friend to work today to ease the monotony," words Luster.

"Well, thanks for asking for permission first," voices the mustached one. "Guys, let's all just start bringing our friends to work to ease the monotony." The younger males laugh.

"Ray, this is my jack-off of a boss named Joe," says Luster. "These are my co-workers Derek and Jared."

Joe. Joe. Mustache, mustache. Eyeballs. Teeth, bone, flesh, hair. It's him. Futon. It's him. Wildcats logo. Him. U.K. cap. It's him! The man! Joe! Futons. Mustache. It's him.

"Ray?" I guess it's Luster that said that. "Ray? Are you okay?"

I run out of the office. Find the closest restroom.

Luster comes in the restroom. As I'm wanting to do something over the sink. I'm a mess.

"What is *wrong*?!" asks Luster.

"It's *him*!"

"Who?!"

"The American of whom's forgiveness I came here for!"

"Who?!"

"Your boss."

A woman comes in. She immediately leaves when she sees us. I picked wrong toilet in my excitement.

"*Joe*?!" asks Luster. "Are you sure?"

"I am nearly positive. I remember those eyeballs. I

remember the pain I caused them. Has he ever talked about being shot in war?"

"I do not know. We have never really talked. Come on. You should go speak to him."

It's too big. I shake head no.

"*Why not?*" mouths Luster.

"I'm scared."

"It could not be half as scary as a war," he says. Strongly he then picks me up and carries me on his shoulder. We leave the ladies room like this.

Luster sets me on my feet. Right in front of Joe. My old victim.

"Look—I don't want your druggie friends comin in here and freakin out on me," says Joe.

"Joe, did you fight in the Persian Gulf War?" asks Luster.

"Hell yeah. Maybe if you weren't so self-centered you would have heard me talking about it. Even took a bullet in the hip. Why?"

"My friend Ray has something he wants to tell you."

Deep breaths. Have to do this. Why I'm here.

"Joe—I–Joe, I–I've rehearsed this moment for years. Our long national nightmare is over. Joe, my name is Ray Fuquay. Joe—"

"Is he on crack?" asks Joe.

"No," says Luster. "Come on, Ray. Just tell him."

"Joe, I am so, so, sorry. I've never been sorrier for anything."

"*What?* What'd you do?" he yells.

"I was the Iraqi soldier who wounded you in war. It was at close range under the Kalzaba bridge in Qasr al-Khubbaz. I'm absolutely positive of it. I am sorry."

Joe looks at me. For some time. He falls back in his chair. He pulls down on his face with both hands, as if thinking or at the end of wits.

"Boys, get out of here. Go fill the orders," he commands. His workers obey, except for Luster.

"You too, Johnson," tongues Joe.

"Joe, you should know about the Christmas peace of World War I," says Luster. Luster loves this story and told it to me many times.

"I read in an alien conspiracy book called *The Gods of Eden* that on Christmas Eve, 1914, a British soldier raised a flag that said 'Merry Christmas.' Soon after, Christmas carols came from the German camp. Soon after that, both armies were hugging each other in no man's land. Germans and Brits were talking together, singing together, and exchanging gifts. The strange peace went on even until the day after Christmas because no one wanted to fire the first shot. The fighting did not—"

"Johnson, shut the fuck up. What the hell do I care?"

"I just thought you would feel more comfortable if you knew something somewhat similar to this had happened before."

"Get to work," orders Joe.

"You better not hurt him," speaks my friend before leaving Joe and me alone.

"I am sorry," I say. "You are why I came to America. I can't believe I've finally found you. I am sorry."

"Have a seat," Joe says with nothing in his face or voice. He stares at me intensively.

"Uh, you realize this is pretty weird for me, don't you?" asks Joe.

"Yes. Me too. But I beg your forgiveness."

"Man. What are the odds of you actually finding

me?"

"I didn't think I ever would. It was Luster who inspirated me onward. He said since I, like he, am not subject to, eh, linear humanoid thought, that I could slip between cracks easier. He says cracks are the best people like us have. He said that fate is friendly toward the freak."

"God. That Luster," he replies. "Talk about freaks."

I laugh nervilously with Joe.

"Heh, heh. Yes. That crazy Luster."

"Man," says dumbfounded Joe. He needs some talking to. I've had the words ready for years.

"I know how you must feel about me and other Middle Easterners. But *please*, don't think of me as the enemy. I want you to know that me shooting you was not out of hatred. I didn't even want to. I love people, and I love the world. And I love your country even more than the world. Forgive me."

Joe rubs his face some more. Silence makes it awkward. He finally speaks.

"Ah, hell. I forgive ya."

"You *do*?!"

"Yeah. Why not? It wasn't that life-threatening of a wound. Put me out of action—that's what hurt the most. Anyhow, you were just doing your job. I can't hold that against ya. Just forget about it."

"Oh, *Joe!*"

I jump up and walk around the desk in order to give him hugs. He doesn't hug me one back, but I don't mind it.

"Okay. Okay. That's enough. Just forget it," he says.

"Joe, is there anything I can do to make up to you? Anything at *all*?"

"Nah. It took some balls to apologize like that. You've

earned your forgiveness."

"Yes!" I say loudly. "Maybe we can go out for frap-puccinos some time."

"Yeah," he says.

"Great," I say.

"Okay then," he says.

"All right then," I say.

I shake his hand.

"Thank you, Joe. Again, I'm very sorry for shooting you."

"Don't worry about it."

XI. We Miss December

Aurora

I've been unusually happy as of late. I think it's because we've been having such a good time here at Ember's house. We've been playing relentlessly every night, making the most of our nice practice space. We get to play as much as we want, and we're really starting to sound good. I don't even know what bands to compare us to or what type of music to call us. I know anyone with a band says that, but I honestly think we defy categorization.

All I can say about us is that we are energetic and raucous, melodic yet heavy, endearing yet revolting, sweet yet brackish, everything simultaneously delivered with a solicitous vengeance. Music is getting old and everything's been done, but I seriously doubt there's ever been an act that has sounded or looked like us. I know exactly what I sound like right now, but I think we have potential to be the greatest thing to happen to music since people heard Elvis on the radio and assumed he was black.

In the last two weeks, we've all become more focused on the band. Especially Ray. His keyboard-guitar playing has drastically improved since he found his man. He still misses his family, but I think he uses the music as a distraction. I think of music as being a distraction with a future.

No matter what goes on during the day with its depraved people and slothful clocks, we always have the night to look forward to. Of course, since I quit working, I haven't had to deal with people or punching clocks. Instead, Opal and I ridicule soap operas and make prank phone calls all day. But just knowing that we will be playing original music at night gives our banal days a sense of worth.

It's usually at around seven that we retreat to the basement and escape into the songs that Luster wrote. We don't reemerge until ten or eleven. We have long practices because we know this won't last. Ember's parents will have to come home eventually, making these four fleeting weeks feel like a childhood Christmas vacation.

So tonight, after three hours of us rocking out, the basement is filled to its capacity with our energy, and after an hour of TV tag, it is now my turn to tell Ember a bedtime story. I'm surprised that she would want to participate in something like that. Of course, she never wants to hear fairy tales or anything like that, stuff she calls "bullshit stories." She only wants to hear stories about us, since I guess we're one of the few things she doesn't hate.

Upon her request, I tell her the story of how I met Luster and Opal, and it goes like this:

"Once upon a time, I was a nudie dancer at a trashy club called the Busy Booty. Actually it wasn't that long ago. About a year ago. It was just another stupid thing I did, another one of my phases. But I did have my reasons for it.

"So anyhow, one night the announcer introduced me like he always did."

"'Gentlemen, straight from the depths of Hell, we have…Aurora!'

"Me being a Satanist started out just as my stage gimmick. I wore horns and a tattered black cloak, and my prop was this nasty male mannequin named Paolo. I always danced to the Misfits song 'Devil's Whorehouse.'

"When I came out on stage that night I was surprised to see this older lady holding up her horn-hands and yelling, 'Yes! Fuckin—A!' She wasn't the typical Busy Booty patron. We usually only got dirty men who looked depressed.

"She was with a young black guy who didn't look too happy about being there. It was, of course, Opal and Luster, out on a date.

"So anyhow, back to my routine. My act was specifically designed to make those dirty men feel as sleazy as they looked and acted. I tried hard not to look sexy. I'd take my cloak off to reveal cryptic body paintings like pentagrams and the words THE LUSTFUL written on my belly, and I'd smear fake blood all over myself. You could hardly even see any flesh even though I was just wearing little black underwear. Also, I'd be shrieking the whole time as if I were in pain. It was supposed to be hideous, but the men usually got off on it anyway. I can't win.

"Another thing is that I didn't even dance. I preferred to think of myself as a performance artist. Instead of gyrating or dry-humping the floor, I'd just float around in circles like I was in the middle of a whirlwind, being blown every which way. And sometimes I'd pick up the mannequin and kind of violently straddle him.

"That night I wandered to the front of the stage close to where Opal and Luster sat. I felt compelled to stare at both of them because I had a feeling they were the only ones in the room who might *get* what I was doing.

"But Luster, being the antagonist that he always is, yelled 'What is she staring at?' I think Opal told him to relax, that I probably just wanted money. She held up a dollar bill to me, and I gave her a dirty look as I took it. I was a little disappointed in her. Then I stared some more at Luster, and he exploded.

"He said, 'What are you staring at, devil woman? I get so sick of you people!'

"Then he got up and left. Opal yelled, 'Oh, get over it!' but he was already out the door.

"After my routine, I put on my nightcloak and headed out of the club. I had to tell my boss I was leaving, and after I did, Opal came up to me. She complimented my act and said that she loved my musical selection, and so did her boyfriend.

"It turns out Luster was mad about being at the strip club in the first place. He hated strip clubs because he thought they were more about commerce than sexuality. It was too fake for his taste. So Opal had dragged him there. She had never been to a strip club and wanted to see what it was like. She loved it there.

"I told her I was sorry that I caused her boyfriend to leave, that I hadn't meant anything by staring at them, and that I felt bad about it. She accepted my apology and said not to pay any attention to Luster because he was always sensitive to how people reacted to seeing him and her together.

"Opal and I left the club at the same time, and Luster was pacing in the parking lot. I was a little scared of him at first. Here's about how our first conversation went:"

Opal said, "Luster, this is Aurora. I got to talking to her, and she wasn't meaning to offend you by staring at us like that."

I said, "Yeah. Sorry if I freaked you out. Our boss

wants us to make eye contact with the patrons. As if they were looking at our *eyes*. Well, *you* were, I guess. But I'm sorry about that."

Opal said, "See. She's all right. She didn't mean nothing."

Then Luster said:

"First off, you did not freak me out. Secondly, I can see right through you. Your flesh is beautiful but transparent. Why do you even bother wearing clothes when you know they will just wind up on the floor?"

I said, "Hey, I apologized for staring at you. What's with the attitude? Just because you have such a bad haircut doesn't mean you have to be a dick to everyone."

Opal laughed. Luster didn't.

He said, "I hate you."

I said, "Take it easy. I was just kidding."

"*Just kidding?* So you were *just kidding?* Like what you said has been totally negated just because you were thoughtful enough to say *just kidding?*"

Opal interrupted, "I'm sorry. He always acts like this, and I'll tell you, Luster, I'm getting sick of it. You better cool it or you can kiss my can good-bye, you smart-ass."

I laughed at Opal for having an attitude that rivaled Luster's. Actually, she *did* end up dumping Luster because of the way he acted with other people when they went out.

He said, "Laugh on, laugher, but my elderly girlfriend and I have found love in each other. I know your pretty head cannot comprehend that."

That really pissed me off, so I spoke up.

I said, "Oh. So I must be stupid because I'm just a stripper slut, right?"

Of course, Luster let me have it.

He said, "Yes. You are a dumbslut. You have been cultivating your dumbslut image since your early teens when your parents divorced. You found the attention you lacked at home in guys giving it to you physically. You are a high school dropout. You were impregnated by a mystery father. To ensure that your child lives well, you became a nudie dancer, which we are supposed to think is so noble. But the truth is, you would be a nudie dancer no matter what. You have spent your whole life teasing men, only dating the assholes who beat you."

Opal yelled at him. "Luster! *Chill!*"

I asked him, "Are you done?"

He wasn't. "Also, you still like Disney cartoon movies."

I wouldn't have argued with him, but he was way off on everything. So I retorted:

"No, I don't like Disney movies, and my parents didn't divorce. My mom died. I'm not a high school dropout, and I don't have a baby. And I know there's no point in my even saying this because no one ever believes me, but I've never even had sex."

I continued: "And I am not a nudie dancer. I am a performance artist. If you had been paying attention, you would have noticed my act tonight was based on Canto Five of Dante's *Inferno*. But I'm guessing you don't read."

That shut him up. He just stared at the ground. Opal said, "Well, shiver me timbers. Luster's speechless." I guess it hadn't happened before.

Luster looked up at me and said, "Canto Five—the damnation of the lustful! 'There is no greater pain than to remember, in our present grief, past happiness.'"

I said, "So you *do* read."

He nodded and said, "Let me get this processed. Your creepy-ass stripping is meant as a lesson to all the horny men who watch you. You are trying to change their lustful ways. Correct?"

He nailed it. I said, "Yes! You're the first person who gets it!"

He said, "That is pretty righteous."

Opal said, "See. She isn't such a dumbslut after all."

"So Luster apologized for the way he had talked to me, and we were friends from then on. He made me admit that I was wasting my time giving lessons in morality at a strip club. A week later I was in my wheelchair. And another week later I met you and Ray. The end."

These stories about us seem to have a soothing, peaceful effect on the beastly Ember. She's asleep with something that may pass for a smile on her little face.

The next day my father calls me. He wants to talk to me in person but doesn't tell me why. He sounds more pissed off than usual.

As soon as I walk in the house, he holds a calendar to my face. I'm shocked to see a picture of myself as Miss December.

"What the hell is *this*?" yells my father.

"Oh my *God*" is all I know to say.

In the picture, I'm sitting on a motorcycle on a beach in a tight black dress, looking seductive but playful. In the background Commander Ken, the fast food chain's long dead founder recently resurrected as a cartoon mascot, walks on the ocean while fried chicken floats around him.

"What is my congregation going to think of this? I can tell them how to live their lives, but I can't even keep my own daughter from being in a girlie chicken calendar! I mean— when Stacy got pregnant was one thing, and when you were a stripper was another, but do you know how many people go to Ken's Fried Chicken?"

"But, Dad, this is fake. David didn't have my permission to do that. I left him when he asked me to pose for that."

"Then how do you explain *this*, Miss December?" He shakes the calendar at my face.

"He obviously used a computer to superimpose me. I swear I've never sat on a motorcycle on the beach, and Commander Ken can't walk on water, either, can he?"

My father throws the calendar on the coffee table. He sits down and sighs.

"God, what have I done to deserve a daughter of such ill repute?"

"I am *not* of ill repute."

"You were a *stripper*, for Christ's sake!"

"I was a *performance artist*."

"How did you get into all this slutty business, anyway? Was it that Luster? Has he been pimping you out?"

"I thought you liked Luster!"

"Oh, I know his kind. All that smooth talking."

It takes an hour, but I finally convince my father that I didn't pose for the calendar, that I'm not a slut, and that I'm still a virgin. He is especially happy to hear that last fact.

"Thank God," he says, hugging his untainted daughter. "I was beginning to worry that I was a complete failure as a father *and* a reverend. You've restored my faith with your morality, Rory."

I don't bother telling him that my virginity has nothing to do with morality, that my frigidity is based on a palpable disgust for fellow man, that I've simply had no desire to consummate any relationship with any of the primitive idiots I've so far encountered in this town, and that so-called morality has been a favorable side effect. I don't bother telling him all that stuff.

Now that he's cooled down, I'm tempted to ask him what he, an honorable reverend, would be doing with a sexy calendar like that. But I let it go. Let him lust after two-dimensional whores. After all, he's only human, and the older I get, the more I find that tired cliché of an excuse to be appropriate.

XII. Molding Young Minds

Ember

I'm always along for the ride. I can't drive. I don't have a choice. But someday I'll be sixteen. Look out when that happens. And then I turn eighteen, and then I turn twenty-one. By that age everything becomes okay. I can do everything.

Aurora drives us to Ken's Fried Chicken. She drives a LeBaron. She's mad about what her ex-boyfriend did. Luster says he did it because he couldn't accept her not being a whore. So he made her one behind her back to make it fit better. Luster says he will take care of it. That's why we're here.

I follow Aurora back to the kitchen of the Ken's Fried Chicken. We see a prettyboy reading a *Maxim* magazine with a slut on the cover.

"Aurora! I know why you're here," says Prettyboy. "You're probably pissed about me putting your picture in the calendar, aren't you? But, hey—you had clothes on in it, so I figured you wouldn't care. So are we cool?"

"Yeah, David. We're cool. That's not why I'm here."

Aurora's ex-boyfriend is a cool guy. A trashy cool guy. Aurora should have known about him. After he looks all over her body, he finally notices me.

"This is my friend Ember," says Aurora.

"Hey, Ember," he says. He offers me a high five. Adults always do that to me. I do not give him one. He doesn't care. He's already looking at Aurora's body again.

"Damn, Aurora. You are lookin tight. You should stand more often. Do you want your wheelchair back?"

"No. Keep it."

"What was that all about anyway?"

"Just another phase I was going through. Anyhow, I came to ask you something."

"Cool."

"I was just wondering, are you more like a floppy disk or a hard drive?"

Aurora keeps David occupied with her questions. Luster makes his move. I'm supposed to keep watch. He's out there talking to the cashier girl. She comes back to the kitchen.

"Duuude. David, that black guy out there wants to buy, like, every calendar we have, man," says the dumb-slut.

"Cool." His face bunches up. "Hey—wait a minute. Aurora, do you happen to know anything about this?"

"No!" says Aurora. She looks out front. Luster is playing with his big hair. "Like I'd have anything to do with *that* guy."

"True," says the dumb-ass. "That's cool. Christy, go ahead and sell all of 'em. Might as well. Better yet, let me sell 'em."

The dick stands up. Then Aurora says, "But, *David,* I'm not through with you yet."

He sits back down and sends the slut off. He only looks at Aurora.

"Are you more like pancakes or waffles?"

A couple minutes later I see Luster leaving. I give my

signal.

"Aurora, I want to go home and listen to the Debby Boone record."

"Wait just a minute, Ember. She loves 'You Light Up My Life,'" says Aurora.

"Shit, no! I want to listen to the Debby Boone record, now! Now or die! Take me!" I throw pans on the floor and scream. It's not as fun since I'm supposed to.

"Okay, okay, okay. Settle down," says Aurora. "Sorry, David. We gotta go."

"Wait, uh, maybe we could go to a club later and do some body shots or something?" says Fuckhead.

"Take me!" I scream.

"Sorry. I gotta go," says Aurora.

"Aight. Call me!" he yells when we are leaving.

A box full of calendars sits next to me in the backseat. Aurora said it would be easy to steal them from that dumb cashier girl. She is a crackhead and always comes to work messed up. Luster paid her in dog-betting vouchers.

Our next stop is the Pandemonium. It is the only rock club in town. It is actually a bar. Many people go there. My parents go there a lot.

I follow Luster in. The club is big and empty since it's daytime. A rock 'n' roll man is sitting at the bar. He reads a *Maxim*. He is young and has a nose ring, a little goatee, tattoos, purple hair, and leather pants.

"Can I help you?" asks the dork. He also has a tongue ring.

"Maybe," answers Luster. "I have a power-pop new wave heavy metal punk rock band named the Anomalies. We want to rock it here like a Randy Savage elbow drop a.s.a.f.p."

"That's cool. You can just give me your name and number, and I'll put you on the list."

"What list?!"

"Dude, there's like, twenty bands from the tri-state area who are waiting to play at my club. This is the place to be on the weekends. So just chill. I'll put your name on the list, and you can wait six months like everyone else."

"But we are not like everyone else, and I have to get the rock rolling to get out of this nightmare of the nine to five. We are ready to play. We are ready to rock this town once and for all, put it behind us, and then embark on a rock odyssey of Biblical proportions. We cannot wait that long. We have a lot of work to do and must get started. We have an eighty-year-old guitarist. We have a bass player whose parents might not let her play here once they return from vacation. It has to be next weekend."

"Man, I'm sorry, but I don't care, dude. Do you want your name on the list or not?"

"Here are ten Ken's Fried Chicken calendars with your name on them. Let us play."

Luster hands the prick the calendars. The prick looks through one of them and laughs.

"Dude, I've boned half of these skanks. Hey, why is December missing?"

"Can we play here this weekend or not?" asks Luster.

"No, dude."

"It seems like you would be more sympathetic," says Luster. "Look at you. You have your piercings and your vinyl pants and your Gen X facial hair. You are what they use to sell Mountain Dew. Your image has been co-opted by corporate America to use in commercials for everything from Starbursts to Volkswagens. They hire models to pose as quirky slackers to sell their stuff, and yet here you are, the genuine article, not seeing a dime. You are being used."

"Fuck you, dude."

"The other day I saw a fifteen-year-old cheerleader with that same tattoo on the small of her back," says Luster.

"All right, man. Now you're never playing here, plus I'm gonna have to kick your ass."

"I knew you would say that, you Dave Navarro mother fletcher," says Luster. "Plan B, Ember. I did not want to resort to this. Please excuse our bass player for one moment."

As I'm leaving, I hear the dork say, "Man, I can't have a fuckin little kid playing here, anyway."

I return with Aurora walking behind me.

"Do we have a gig or not, Luster?" she says. "I'm getting tired of waiting in the car."

"This pecker says we have to wait six months to play here like everyone else."

He's already looking at her all over.

"Whoa, whoa, whoa, wait a minute," he says. "*She's* in your band?"

We have a gig next Friday. I hope I grow up to be pretty. It will make my hell-raising much easier.

Monday I get in trouble again at school. The lesbo teacher couldn't get my parents to come in for another conference. They are bungee-jumping in Cancun.

The teacher says it's important. She calls my emergency contact, Opal. Opal comes in after school to talk to her. Ray is with her. I sit on the floor.

"First, I guess I should show you Ember's latest stunt," says Ms. Watson.

She shows Opal and Ray the flyer I made. It shows a naked demon licking another naked demon. It says "Live @ The Pandemonium, Friday—The Anomalies." I got caught passing it out to the other kids.

"That's us!" says Ray. "We're the Annohmaylees."

"It's the *AnnAHmullies*, dipshit," says Opal.

Luster came up with our name the other day. I looked it up. It's perfect for us. Nobody knows what it means.

"Yeah. Ember's in that band with us. She's publicizing our show with a punk rock flyer. What of it?" asks Opal.

"Ms. Oglesby, the picture on the flyer is entirely inappropriate. Furthermore, do you really think Ember should be allowed to play with you adults at this establishment? I've heard it gets pretty wild there."

"Well, furthermore even more, it's an all-ages show," says Opal. "We wanted it that way. And take it from me, fellow. You're only young once. I wish I had been rocking out at her age."

Opal has taught me to rock out every chance I get.

"You should come see us," says Ray. "We rock it—oh we rock so goodly, it is like—can I say 'orgasmic' as a word?"

"I'm sorry, who are you?" asks my teacher.

"I'm friends with Ember and Opal. I am here for supporting morals."

"I see. Well, since I last met with Ember's parents, I've seen no improvements in her behavior. In fact, in the last three weeks, it's gotten worse. It's almost like she's *trying* to get sent home."

"No shit," I say. They don't hear me or act like they

don't.

"We know all about her behavior," says Ray. "We can't get her to go to bed until little hours like two or three. We have to tell her bedtime stories to get her to wake down. But she's not hurting anything or anyone. She is being Ember. We think it is okay."

"So are you *living* with Ember?" asks the teacher.

"The whole band lives with her, just until her parents return," says Ray. "The band has practice at Ember's every night, and then we all just sleep over for slumber partying."

"Shut up, Ray," says Opal. "She doesn't need to hear about all of that."

"That would explain why she's been falling asleep so much lately," says Ms. Watson. "She's also been breaking the dress code, dressing like Tina Turner from *Mad Max* nearly every day."

"We thought that was cute," says Opal.

"I'll give you the bottom line. Ember's stretched this school's rules and regulations to their limit. The principal has decided to expel her. And considering her parents aren't even in this country and that she is living with a rock band, I will *have* to recommend that she be put in the East Home."

"Actually, expelling her would work out nice for us," says Opal. "We were thinking about going on tour soon, so that would free her bum-bum up."

"But a child needs an education, and—"

"I know that. Let me finish, boy! Could we home-school her on the road?"

"I don't think so."

"We're sure not gonna let you put her arse in some home. Her parents may not be worth a crud, but she's got family in us."

Opal strokes my hair. Ray pats me on the shoulder. Being expelled sounds okay. I hate school and the people in it. I am happy with this situation. I like being expelled.

We had a good three weeks together. But this week is not all that great. We don't know what's going to happen to me. We've been avoiding the people from the girls' home. Opal and I mostly stay in the basement and don't answer the door.

Also, Aurora's ex-boyfriend won't leave her alone. He found out she was here. But we have caller ID. We finally took the phone off the hook. Aurora also stays in the basement.

Luster and Ray miss the meals sometimes this week. They go out to pass out flyers and tell people about the show. They come home to practice and sleep.

We are tense about the show. We wonder if we're good enough. Many times this week, Ray has vomited. I stand by him in the bathroom sometimes as he pukes.

Luster says everything should work out if we do well Friday. (I doubt this.) He says if we're a hit, and maybe even if we're not, he'll set up a tour. We can play all over this country. Maybe someday the world. I want to kick ass in a good way if I can.

XIII. All Together Now

Luster

Tonight is as crucial to our lives as our mothers' vaginas. Shoulder demons whisper to me, though I cannot differentiate their voices. I cannot distinguish between the timbres of the ideal realist Richard Dreyfuss or the real idealist Albert Camus. None the nevertheless, tonight could tell us everything we need to know about our future as rock music road warriors on the seven chunk ball Earth. Tonight is a microcosm. If they hate us at the biggest club in a small town, they'll hate us at the smallest club in the biggest town. If the small reptile minds out there can accept us, then I will have faith in all the rest.

We are backstage, already in costume but about to tear our diversified flesh off. My bandmates sit on a couch before me. I talk to myself as I so often do to ease my mind and to get to know me better, though my dramatic monologue is intended for them as well.

If you are not nervous, you should be. Cowardly are the cool. Coolness comes from lies that people give themselves—that they are in control, that everything is going to be all right, that they belong wherever they are. The truth is that every second of every day, there are a thousand things that could go wrong, from the tiny animals infecting our bloodstream to the biggest VIPs making horrendous mistakes that will make our great-grandchildren want to sleep all day. The same applies to our show tonight.

"Is this supposed to be a pep talk?" asks Aurora.

No. I am no coach. I am not that big of an asshole. I am just talking so that my thoughts make sounds. The same principle makes me love rock music. But even rock goes wrong sometimes. I have the highest of hopes for us, hopes that hop on pogo sticks atop the Olympus Mons. But remember who we will be playing for tonight: humanoids, monkeys with wardrobes. Just by looking at us, they might not like us, but it is only fair as I do not like them. Our only chance of getting through is our sound, so you had better play well. Play like you are going to die. This is my dream, so do not botch it. I do not ever want to start hating you. You are four people I never want to add to my two-century-long shit list.

Club Owner

Dude. This crowd is fucked up. We usually get, like, twenty-something white dudes and their girlfriends. Tonight we're getting everything from old people to little kids. Now I know why that hot chick's band wanted it to be all-ages, since it must be their crowd. But it's not just their ages. I'm seeing everything from big black dudes to rednecks to teenagers to well-dressed adults to strippers I've boned to preps and even a lesbian.

It's fucked up, but I can't complain. There's a shitload of people here, and I don't care what *they* look like because their cash all looks the same. I should start having all-ages shows, and I should probably even have that one band play here regularly.

I go backstage, and there they are. I almost crack up

laughing at 'em 'cause of their goofy outfits. They're in these shiny glittery gold jumpsuits with tassels on the sleeves and pant legs. That's actually pretty cool. It's nice to see a band going all out for a change.

"Whuzup?" I say to the hot chick.

"Hey," she says and smiles. She wants me.

"You guys go on in ten minutes. Do you need anything? A Heineken or something?"

"No thanks," she says.

"Cool. We have a kick-ass crowd out there tonight. Probably the biggest I've seen since Stranger Danger came to town."

"We *oughtta* have a big crowd out there," says the old lady. "Luster and Ray have been promotin it like a son of a bitch this past week. They flyered the fuck out of this show."

"Cool," I say, making sure my sleeves are rolled high enough for the hot chick to see my tattoos/muscles.

That prissy foreign dude peeks through the curtains.

"Ooh! Almond joy!" he yells. "He's right. There are tons o' people in the attendance. Hey! Joe is here!"

Must be his boyfriend.

"So you want to come to a party at my bachelor's pad after the show?" I ask the chick.

"No. I'm sorry, but I hate parties."

"That's cool." There went your next gig at my club, bitch.

Ray

Making my way through the crowd. So varying! What beautiful melting pots you can get in this country! Leather, denim, hair dye, pants, every sort of haircut all over everywhere. Teenage boys make me think of Aymon. Wish he was here. If success comes, Milkah will take me back. They will come back to me, to live to the best.

But all of the different types look at me funny because of my rock and roll costume. I "excuse me" all the way through them all until I get to Joe in the middle of teen people. He looks bored, smokes droopy cigarette, and wears John Deere cap.

"Joe!" I yell.

"What's up?" he speaks, looking at my outfit. Smells like beer.

"I'm so glad you came here! I got you a present!" I had his present specially made. It is a T-shirt. A nice one! (Airbrushed.) He holds it up to read the front.

"'I fought in the Gulf War, and all I got was this lousy T-shirt.' Ha. That's pretty good. Course I also got a bullet in the hip, thanks to you! Still limp a little! Got sent home and couldn't finish my duty as an American!"

How? Don't know what to say. But then he starts laughing friendily, so so do I.

"Just kidding," he says.

Brother

Shit. I see a bunch of familiar mothah fuckas up in here, you know whum sayin. Cuz I've fuckin sold weed to half the mothah fuckas in here, aight. And acid, shit, ecstasy, occasional meth, whatevah, know whum sayin. Wait 'til I tell 'em 'bout my crack, you know whum sayin. It's all good. My little brothah wanted me to come to this shit, you know whum sayin. Fuckin told us all to come. We said, shit, we didn't want any of that freaky shit, you know whum sayin. He fuckin told us off, said we was— what was it?— that Eve record, yeah, Eveolution. Said comin here was the least we could do cuz we was makin Eveolution go backwards or something, know whum sayin. Said we was, shit, fuckin turnin back into apes and shit right before his eyes like those mothah fuckas went from pigs to men in *Animal Farm* or some shit. Fuckin quotin books and shit we don't know about. Sometimes I wanna bust a cap in his smart ass, you know whum sayin. His *Reading Rainbow* ass, you know whum sayin. We didn't know what the fuck he was talkin 'bout, you know whum sayin, but we came cuz we figured we could find some customers here, and we was right.

Aurora

As I'm looking over the crowd through the curtains, I see that my father ended up coming to the show. He's gradually coming to terms with his broken Jesus statue, and I think he no longer resents the band. I see him out there talking to Christy and Kristie. He probably recognizes them from the calendar.

I also happen to see an odd-looking boy standing alone off to the side. He looks uncomfortable here but kind of like he'd be uncomfortable regardless of his surroundings. He's looking at the crowd like he either hates them or he's afraid of them, or maybe even afraid for them. He's not handsome in a traditional sense, and I could do without the dorky Bill Cosby sweater, but I want him horribly. I'm picturing him nervously approaching me after we play a perfect set, and he'd say something like, "I'm sorry, but y'all's music is just so gorgeous that it hurts me to watch you play it," or "I've been looking for someone like you for so long that I had already given up," or "Please love me. It could be you and me versus everyone."

Then, from behind me, I hear someone remark "Whuzup?" in a cool guy voice. It's David. He's wearing a visor and jeans with slits cut at the bottom so the pant legs can drape casually over his sandals.

"What are you doing back here?" I ask him.

"Just chillin. I'm here to forgive you. I've been trying to call you. I know you and that black dude stole my calendars. But hey, I guess I had it coming, you know whum sayin, and I can't stay mad at you when you're lookin so fine. So are we cool?"

"Sure. I gotta go do something." I attempt to leave, but he keeps talking.

"Cool. Tell you what. Just to show you there are no hard feelings, I'll let you hang out with me sometime."

"Don't do me any favors, David."

"That's cool. Man, lately, you are such a hotty. I gotta be honest, I'm sweatin you pretty hard. What are you doing after the show?"

"I don't know."

"Let's hook up."

"David, I'm sorry, but I'm not interested. I don't know why I ever was. You're a typical male. You're a dick. Please leave me alone."

"That's cool."

I walk away. Even after what he did to me with the calendars, I still feel bad about talking to him like that. But with these horny, cocky guys and their one-track minds, sometimes you gotta get tough and s-p-e-l-l things out to get through to them. Even cool guys have to get their hearts broken sometimes. Don't they?

Ex-Boyfriend

Nobody has ever done this to me. She cannot do this to me. Stupid bitch. She cannot treat me like that. I'm not some teenage boy you can just brush off. I'm a man, point blank. I'm twenty-three, I'm in my prime, I got girls all over my stick, I've backpacked across Europe, I got a cool job, a sweet Jeep, tight body, perfect hair, people love me, and you don't talk to me like that. Stupid bitch. I'm gonna make her pay. She's a hot piece of ass, but you know what? So am I. The bottom line is you don't treat *me* like that, point blank…Ah cool, somebody's got a sweet amp back here. It would kick ass as a car stereo speaker. Cool.

Opal

I see some prettyboy snooping around my amp, probably dreaming about what it would be like to have car speakers that size. I say, "That's not a bass amp like you'd want, so just fuck off," and he says "whatever" and does just that.

I peek through the curtains to take a look-see at the

audience. It's a damn good-sized crowd. For once in my eighty years living here, this town has surprised me. I see most everyone I know, except for my nieces and their kids. I see my group therapy cronies, and even Kip took the night off from the gay bar to come and see me. Lots of sweet prat out there, too.

Dammit. I wish I had been rockin out all along like this instead of working in a damn car part factory my whole life, slaving away making rims and hubcaps. But I reckon I can make up for it now. I'll just rock extra hard.

I hope the show goes well tonight. Ah, what the hell— Dear Lord, please let it go well tonight at the show. Let them accept us and like us. And please let us get somewhere with our music. We all need it. I'm sorry I haven't talked to you for so long or gone to church for ten years, but it's just 'cause I didn't want to be partying and having sex on a Saturday just to be acting all holy on Sunday. You know that's what they all do, and I didn't want to be like that. I'm sorry. And you know every time Mass was over and everyone was filing out, they wouldn't let each other out of the pews and into the aisles. There were similar situations in the parking lot afterwards. It just got to the point where I hated being around those people, and then I got so old that I started doing whatever I wanted. Isn't that sorta like you?

Come to think of it, could that explain things? I know you waited millions of years before you put us here. Were you just getting tired by that point, and that's why we turned out like this, so used up and unoriginal? I don't mean to blame you, and I should point out that you have made a few diamonds in the rough. Russell Crowe and Wesley Snipes immediately come to mind. And you did really well with my bandmates, too.

I hope we do you proud, because we really are on a kind of mission with this band, and I think it's one that you'd approve of. Anyhow, I thank you for everything. It's been rough, but here I am, so thanks for letting me be. Please, just don't let me start driving slow like an old woman anytime soon, and please let things go well tonight.

G o d

Opal:

Thank you for submitting your query for "THINGS GOING WELL TONIGHT AT THE SHOW." However, We are currently experiencing a heavy production schedule, and, unfortunately, your project does not meet Our needs at this time. Thanks for considering Us, and best of luck to you tonight and in the future.

Yours Truly,

God

P.S.–You're right about Crowe and Snipes. They're a couple of my faves, too!

E m b e r

I had another nightmare last night. Everybody was dying. It was no one I knew. Just tons of people without faces. Billions of them. All of them. Their faces were cut off. They were in piles. They were on fire.

I was safe, though, up really high somewhere. I was telling them to line up and then walk into the fire. They all did exactly what I told them to do.

I watched it all. I was crying tears made of blood. But the scary part was that they were happy tears.

"Are you okay, crazy baby?" asks Luster.

"Yeah."

"You look a bit more saturnine than usual, little friend."

"I'm okay."

Luster crouches down to talk to me. He quiets his voice for me.

"What is wrong, rabid child? Talk."

I can't avoid him, but I don't mind it.

"I'm scared."

"What are you scared of, darling one?"

I can't tell him about my nightmare. It's too weird. Even for him. I don't answer.

"Is it our show? Is that it?" he asks. My dream is bothering me, but he's right. I'm afraid of the show, too. I nod.

"I am scared, too, baby. There would be something wrong with us if we were not scared. We do not want to play it all cool like a bunch of rappers or contestants on *Elimidate* or fratboys at a pool party, do we?"

"No. They're in denial."

Luster laughs. "That is right. You said it." He suddenly frowns. "But, Ember, maybe we were wrong in having you rock out with us. Maybe you should be doing little kid things instead of playing with us."

"No! Hell no, dumb-ass! I'm doing what I want! I love this band! Shuts the hell up, shit-head." The other bandmates walk over when they hear me yelling. Luster doesn't see that they stand behind him. He laughs again.

"There is the Ember venom I know and love." He leans in closer to me and says, "I love this band, too, you know. Even if everyone botches my compositions out there, no matter what happens, I love you people. I guess we really should not be scared after all."

"Ahhh," our bandmates say. He hops up and faces them. "I was having a private conversation with Ember! And what is with that 'Ahhh' shit? This is not an episode of *Full House*. I am not a fucking Olsen twin. And if I meant for all of you to hear—"

Luster keeps yelling. Then they surround him. They hug him and tell him they love him, too.

He finally shuts up.

Therapist

A cute guy comes out on stage. I'm just *crazy* about his outfit! It's so *wild*! Pleather pants, shiny shirt, and those piercings and tattoos! Actually, my little stepsister has a tattoo just like one he has! *Crazy*!

"What's up, mothah fuckas?" he asks.

Oh. Everybody, even the little kids, is yelling "Woo!" so I join in.

"Woo!"

He continues: "How many of you feel like humans?"

Everyone "woos."

"And how many of you feel like fucking animals?"

Everyone "woos," even more than before.

"Later on tonight we got Assficksi8, Hyber Nation, and Spazm. But right now, we got the debut of a brand-new band. Put your hands together for the Anna Mollies!"

Hmm...I like that name. The crowd sort of gives them a hand, and the curtain opens. There's Opal! I *love* the matching gold outfits. The spotlights are causing them to shine. Emilio sleeps in a similar outfit. I notice that quite a few of the people around me are laughing and making fun of them. (Their costumes and them as people.)

That black guy is *crazy*! He won't stop moving. San Francisco. He keeps running back and forth across the stage with his hands in the air. He should be on Broadway! I can't keep my eyes off of him, and it's not because I'm totally gay! Meanwhile, I look at all of my patients, and they are staring in awe at Opal.

I guess if she's not in a nursing home (which I'm convinced she needs to be after hearing her panty-sniffing story! *Gross!*) this is the next best place for her to be with all this craziness!

Cop

The first thing I see and hear when I come in is that crazy Johnson boy running around on stage. I said I'd keep an eye on him, and he's making it easy for me.

"It is *Anomalies*! The *Anomalies*!" he screams into the microphone. "I see a lot of good-looking widows, orphans, introverts, extroverts, latchkey kids, amputees, and Jewish carpenters out there tonight! My name is Luster Johnson, and I am doing well! I am not going to ask you all how you are doing, because I am sure you would just reply by yelling, 'Wooo!'"

A bunch of the audience yells "Woo!" anyway. Ha. I see his brothers are here, too. Must be looking for some customers, and I know about the crack.

"Humanoids, Huey Lewis, I have got news. Tonight

we plan to rock you into oblivion! So blow out your candles, and make a death wish! Unzip the name brand epidermis! Let the razor blade sounds of my crazy trachea cut the cord on the back of your necks!"

Listen to all that. And he ain't on drugs?

Punk

Man, if I've got something to say, I'll just come out and say it. I just don't care.

"Dude, your outfits are fucking gay!" I get a laugh from my buds. I rule. That black dude thinks he's some kind of rock star or something, so fuck him and his friends. I don't get this band. They don't belong here, and they don't belong together.

"Fuck you! I made these outfits!" yells the old lady. The crowd cheers for her. Whatever. Shouldn't she be in a nursing home or something? I give her the middle finger. I don't care if she is an old lady. I don't give a fuck. My friends are lovin it. I'm the man.

The black dude looks right at me. "I cannot believe it!" he says. "A punk rock kid giving the middle finger? What next, asshole? Are you going to accuse us of being sell-outs?"

"Sell-outs!" I yell at him.

"Let me tell you, Punky Punkerson, you can make fun of our outfits until the fat ladies come home and the cow sings. Free is the man who does not mind looking stupid!" he says. "But you probably already knew that!"

Before I threaten to kick his ass, the sweet-ass drummer stands up and yells, "Come on, Luster! Let's play a song!"

Some dude yells, "Show us your tits!" Another dude yells, "That drummer's fucking hot!" Another dude yells, "So is the bass player!"

The bass player is, like, a little girl. After hearing that, she comes up to the edge of the stage and spits at the audience. That is pretty punk rock. So you know what? She's all right.

Hippie

Duuude, maaaan. This black dude's killing my buzz, man. He keeps, like, fucking with everybody. That's so not cool, dude. This is all about meeting new people. It's all about the music, man. Why won't they play some tunes, man?

"I think there are a lot of guys here with small penises but firm handshakes!" See, there he goes again, man. That's, like, not cool, man. I'm fucking high. "I have not seen a crowd this raucous since Sherman Hemsley's Presidential Gala! Maybe you do not deserve our watch-a-macallit rock!"

Dude, man, dude, man, I don't even give a fuck anymore. Phish. I go up to the front and I'm like, "Dude, man, play some tunes, dude. That's not cool."

"Oh, I am sorry. Am I killing your buzz? Well, this will really bring you back down. What you call a counter-culture, I call an excuse to get high and not bathe. In two years you will trade in your sandals for loafers, and I will be hiring you as my accountant."

So not cool, man. How could the crowd be laughing

at him, man? "Dude, man, were you dropped as a baby?!" I say to him. It's all I could think of, man.

"Whoa! Hold on!" he says. "'*Were you dropped as a baby?*' That cut-down is older than poetry!"

Duuude, the crowd keeps laughing, man.

"What next? Is my mother a snowblower? Dost she wear combat boots?"

Man, fuck this crowd laughing, dude. That punk rock dude is next to me. He's like, "Man, fuck that dude. He's a crackhead. Don't pay any attention to him," and he pats me on the back, so I say, "Thanks, man. That's cool."

The punk rock guy and I are gonna smoke a bowl later. And that's what it's all about. Meeting new people and making new friends. And the music.

Teacher

This is getting ridiculous. I'll admit it, I am a very impatient person. I wish they'd play. I told my partner I'd be home by eleven. Hey. Kip's here. I figured he'd be at the bar with Emilio and the gang.

"This song is entitled Honorable Discharge," announces the African-American. What a sick title. "Two, four, six, eight!"

So they finally begin playing. I have to admit, they're actually pretty good. Really loud, upbeat, and strong sounding. Intense, yet melodic. Unique.

"Sometimes men and women make mistakes. And nine months later, they develop when the water breaks." (I think that's what the African-American is singing.)

Ember looks so cute, even though she's trying hard

not to. She's staring at the audience like she's possessed. She's playing that big guitar really hard, so good for her. You go, girl.

Maybe I was wrong. Maybe this is good for her. She can get rid of some of that frustration on stage. It seems to be healthy.

Ex-Boyfriend

Man, I hate to say it, but they rock. I mean, I'm almost feeling bad for what I did. Aurora's still on my mind, but damn, that old girl is looking pretty good, too, as weird as that sounds. She's up there kicking ass on that guitar with her legs spread apart.

The crowd is getting into it. There's a good vibe in the air, and I can't help but bob my head to the music.

Father

I'm so proud of my daughter. I had no idea she could play drums that well. Her hair and arms fly all around her, with her beautiful form in the middle. It is a fast song, but she's keeping the beat perfectly.

Her band exhibits a delightful spunk in its passionate delivery of hard, thrusting rock. And the crowd is loving it! It's only taken a minute, and they've already been won over. The audience is starting to move around and up and down to the music.

The song ends and the venue unleashes a load of

approval in the form of cheers and applause. Some audience members hold their arms erect to display their enthusiasm. I turn to the comely young ladies that stand next to me, old colleagues of my daughter's.

"That's my daughter up there!" I yell. "And they're good!" The young ladies nod in agreement.

"Yes! I can already see some of the brain wires retracting!" enthusiastically yells Luster after the applause finally dies down. I don't know what he's talking about, but he's obviously very happy. He continues:

"As F. Scott Fitzgerald would have said, 'I am thankful to have an existence at all, if only as a reflection in your wet eyes.'"

Another song commences. I see the crowd moving together with smiles on their faces, and I really do think something positive is going on here tonight. God is really into what they're doing. Pubes.

C o p

I'll be damned. I don't know why, but the crowd seems to be enjoying it. Sounds like a bunch of noise to me.

B o s s

I can see him up there playing that gay-lookin keyboard guitar-like thing, but I'm really not hearing what they're doing. If Johnson's the leader, I'm sure it's a bunch of freaky alternative shit, so screw it. I'm in the zone. I'm able to block out all the noise, just like in the war. Besides, I didn't come here to listen to no music.

The bottom line is that I have an opportunity that no man ever gets. My enemy, the man who took me out of action (and a fucking towelhead no less), has presented himself to me on a goddamn silver platter. I'm doing what any red-blooded American male would do if he had the chance. Like they say, payback's a bitch.

Brother

Shit. I gotta say, my little brother rules, you know whum sayin. So this is what he's been doin in our room, writing songs in those notebooks and shit. It's fuckin hype shit, too, you know whum sayin. I mean, it ain't, like, what I'd bump up to in my ride, know whum sayin, but it's still straight though. Bling bling. He's up there dancin all silly and shit, all over the shit. I love it. Has a straight, loud voice, too. Crowd feels it, you know whum sayin. I'm all about love, know whum sayin. Yeah. Yeah. Uh-huh. Yeah. Shit. Mothah fuckin redneck pulling a gun out. Shoots that foreign dude's keyboard. Music stops. Shoots him again. Foreign dude's down. Everybody screaming. I get mine out. Jerome gets his. We cap the redneck's ass just in case, you know whum sayin. Everybody's running out screamin and shit. The show's over.

XIV. Doing His Job

Ray

What is a happening? I don't understand. Noises not good. Sounded like war. Bleeding so freely. Ceiling tiles, black sky. Ambulance. I bleed freely.

My testicles. He got my area. It was him. I saw him. It was Joe. He didn't forgive it after all.

The end of the story flashes in my brain. The Germans and the British. Both their commanders threatened the peace with treason. The fighting resumed. And that's an order.

Luster up above.

"Tell the wife and kid I love them. Tell them I'm sorry I stayed behind here. Sorry 'bout this. Good-bye."

"Do not talk like that, Ray. You were shot in the nuts. You will get through this, and we are going with you," he mouths.

"Oh no you're not, mother fucker!" speaks a man voice somewhere. "No one except the foreigner is going anywhere." Luster leaves cursing.

The foreigner is taken away.

Cop

So at least I got one Johnson where I want him, the crazy

one. I still don't believe that his brothers were totally inno-cent with what went on earlier, even if the witnesses claimed that Joe shot first. Still, I'll get to the bottom of this and book them soon enough. But for right now, I got this one to deal with.

"What the fuck is this all about, cop in a doughnut shop?" asks Johnson.

"We have reason to believe that your band is in pos-session of an illegal substance."

"*What*?"

"We know you got the drugs."

"False!"

"Give it up, Johnson. One of your buddies ratted on you. You're finished. Now gimme the drugs!"

"Sweet shit! I do not have any drugs!"

"Oh, come on, Johnson. We get a call saying you guys have a bag of crack. Then a foreigner gets shot. The two go together. It's a textbook example of a drug-related crime. Your brothers were even here to have your back. Now hand over the drugs, mother fucker!"

"Battleship sunk!" he yells. "Have you ever seen a man's dreams dissipate in five minutes? It is one thing to get shot at, but then to be accused of *this* malarkey. Our injury has been insulted."

Poor ol' Joe. They're rolling him past us. He was a good man, a man's man, and a damn hard worker. I don't know why in the world he would get caught up in a mess with these heathens. Somebody's gonna pay for it.

Opal

The girls and I are still in shock. Ember's on my lap, crying for the first time since I've known her. Being the oldest, I feel like I should say something.

"I think the show was going really well 'til Ray got shot."

"Totally," says Aurora sadly.

The cop and Luster walk over.

"If you ain't talkin, I'll just find the stuff myself," says that cop who interrupted our practice, that one with the mustache and buzz cut. "All of you stay right there. Don't even think about going anywhere." He walks off toward the stage.

"How's Ray?" Aurora asks Luster.

"If this were a movie, you would just say, '*Is he...?*' and not finish your sentence, and then I would interrupt you, as if the audience should be sheltered from the word 'dead.'"

"Come on, Luster. Now's not the time for that crap," I say.

Luster looks embarrassed, which is rare for him.

"He should be okay," he says. "He was shot in the scrotum, but he is still conscious. Right now, we have another problem on our hands with that cop."

"What's going on?" asks Aurora.

"He thinks we have drugs. He thinks that is what the shooting was over. He says someone called and ratted on us."

Oh, shit. Ember looks up at me, probably thinking the same thing—oh, shit.

I can't just not say anything.

"Uhh, I should probably tell y'all something," I whisper.

"What?" asks Luster.

"I just remembered I have a big bag of crack in the back of my amp."

"*What?*" hoots Aurora. Luster stares at me.

"I'm just kind of hiding it from the person that stole it," I say.

"Who stole it?" Aurora asks.

"Well, uh. . ." Ember looks up at me, then at the others, her face still red and moist from crying. She slowly raises her hand. Sorry, Mom and Dad. I've failed as a babysitter. Guess I wouldn't have made that great of a parent after all, dammit.

Ex-Boyfriend

Dude, I guess I wasn't the only one that had it out for that band. It's been a rough night for 'em. But you know, they shouldn't have fucked with me, 'cause that's something you just don't do. Aurora's got a sweet ass and a band that rocks, but you just don't treat me like that and get away with it, stealing my calendars and then shutting me down like that...I'll be cool to you as long as you're cool to me, you know whum sayin, and she was not cool to me.

I see my cop bud looking around on stage, so I sneak around backstage.

"Pssst. What's up, Officer?"

"Hey. What's up, David?"

"Just chillin'. Haven't seen you 'round my Ken's Fried Chicken for a while."

"Yeah. Been busy. What you doing here?"

"Actually, I'm the one who called. I'll show you where

I found their stash."

Aurora

I knew we should've been keeping a closer eye on Ember. I guess we were all caught up in our own stupid problems with the "humanoids," like me with that David prick. I should never have let my guard down for someone like him, someone so average.

"Ember, how could you?" I ask.

"Luster's brothers were being mean to all of us that one night. No one was looking. So I took a bag."

Oh. I remember. Luster's brothers were too busy hitting on me to notice their precious crack was being stolen by an eight-year-old. And I was too busy being hit on.

"She didn't even know what she was stealing," says Opal.

"Yes I did!"

"She showed it to me, and I took it from her," says Opal. "I know I should've thrown it away."

"Why didn't you?" I ask.

"Well, you know how I am. I'll try anything once. I was saving it in case I ever felt the urge. I never felt it, though. Shit. I'm sorry."

"But who would call the police on us?" I ask. Nobody knows. I always felt everybody was out to get us. I guess I was right.

The cop returns with a large Ziploc bag full of what I presume to be crack cocaine. It's yellowish white.

"I'm only going to ask you all once. Whose is it?"

For once, we are silent.

Ember

I cried sad tears for Ray. They needed out. But now I'm mad again. I hate cops. Especially this one.

"Come on, Johnson! Am I going to have to arrest all four of you?"

He can't do this to Luster. I'm the one that ruined everything. I hop off Opal's lap and scream at the cop.

"Don't blame Luster! It's my crack! I stole it. Luster had nothing to do with it!"

The cop looks down at me and smiles. Like adults always do. Now Opal stands.

"Hush, Ember. It's mine, officer. I didn't smoke any of it, but it was in the back of *my* amp."

The cop laughs at her.

"Ma'am, little girl, that's really sweet of y'all, but who are you kidding? What would *you two* want with a bag of crack? Meanwhile, not only was Johnson acting high as a kite on stage, but his family has a history of being arrested for selling drugs. Give it up, Johnson. Y'all can't fool me."

"The policeman is right," says Luster. He sounds soft and calm. "Whom are we kidding? He has to have it his way. He has to make things right. He has the way things are in his head, and he has the uniform to make them be. So, yes, that is *my* crack. Arrest my ass, if that is the way it has to be. Take me away." He holds out his hands to the cop.

"*Luster!*" we all scream. Luster looks at me and smiles like a little kid. The cop is already cuffing him. I cling onto Luster's leg.

"He's lying, officer! Don't you dare arrest him!" yells Opal.

"Ladies, please. I'm just doing my job. Now stand back."

The cop pushes me away. He leads Luster off by the arm. Opal, Aurora, and I stare helplessly. We miss our men.

Luster turns around and smiles. He tries to wave good-bye but has cuffs on. So he kind of wiggles his fingers at us. He turns back around. We hear him yell at his all-time loudest, "Just doing his job! Paying his bills! Nothing personal!"

He had always hated it when people said things like that.

XV. Six Epilogues

Husband

Everything back to normal is comfortable. Back where I belong is good for my health. No more punchings, beatings, and shootings. Peace!

I'm looking similar to other Iraqis and treated the same. Got my routine down and no more surprises. But I still get a feeling when I pull up to my house. I guess the opposite feeling of how I felt that night before I went on stage those months and months ago. But no more of that. The future is what's for dinner.

After another day of work at the sandal factory, I walk in the house to see the wife kitchened, bunned up, and aproned, making our house smell like home.

"Hey, honey. How was the work today?" she asks, tongued Arabically.

"Eh, shitty as usual," I answer. Also tongued Arabically.

We got a stable dinner table. Still the fighting, but not as big. Aymon is behaving and toning back down his clothings. Not so funky now.

Fork, knife, spoon, shut up. Can't stand the silence, so I break it.

"Aymon, how was school today?"

"I still hate it. Nobody likes my kind of music. Nobody understands me."

His talk reminds me of Aurora, who won't write me back.

"Things will get better," says the wife. "You are at an awkward age. Soon you will grow a beard, and life will become less confusing."

Milkah might be right. Once I got back here and regrew the beard, life did become less confusing. I want to add on to the support by showing my son he is not alone.

"Don't feel bad, Aymon. I have been experiencing a similar situation at my work. I make mix tapes of rock music for peers. When I ask them if they like what they hear, they pretend like they don't hear me or even leave the room."

Aymon nods. "Yeah, it's like, nobody here gets it, you know what I am saying?"

"I know what you are saying," I reply.

"Fine! Both of you can go back to America with the infidels and get shot at!" shouts the wife. She won't let me forget that I left a nut in America. She runs away from the table. I try to stop her.

"But, dear, I left it all behind to be with you! Dear— Ahh, screw it."

This happens every once in a few, usually when we talk about U.S.A. things. She gets over it after a few minutes of alone time. Aymon and I keep eating.

"Father, do you miss America?"

I think fatherly with thought before answering.

"I miss my friends. But they were not your typical Americans. They didn't shoot me. Do *you* miss America?"

"Yes. I miss playing music with my friends."

"Me too."

I write these friends of mine but never get written back to. I don't understand. Maybe they think I should've stayed. But what I had to do I had to do I had to do. After what happened, Milkah felt for me. She was willing to take me back. I knew it was time to return. Besides, the way things were heading, the band could be no more with or without a Ray Fuquay.

"And I miss the girls who were allowed to wear such slutty clothes," continues Aymon.

"Oh, yes! Slutty clothes!" I didn't want to show him this, but I can't resist. I raise up my boring cream-colored shirt to reveal my Budweiser halter-top underneath. "Don't tell your mother!"

"I won't." He is proud of me. I can see it in his eyebrows.

"Ooh! Do you know what else I miss?" I ask. "The language. I was just getting the hang of it before I left."

I'm going to do something I haven't done in a very long while. I'm going to switch back to English.

"I wonder if I can still speak English."

"You can!" says Aymon in English. "Hey! I can too!"

"I remember when Luster was helping me with English. He said the worst mistake I could make in speaking the language was starting a sentence with—what was it? ...Ah yes...'With all due respect' or 'Could you do me a favor?'"

We share laughter.

"I wish I could've met your friends," says Aymon.

"I do too."

My wife reminds us this is an Arabic household when she shrieks from her bedroom, "What's that I hear you speaking in there?!"

"Nothing, dear! Come and eat with us!" I say Arabically.

I hear her coming back, but I need to say a little more

English to my son. I know this will be the last time I get to speak the crazy language for a while. So I try to make it something good. I lean in closer to him and whisper.

"Remember, you can always *think* in English. No one would ever know. Besides, nobody ever says the words in their heads anyway."

Grandmother

I hope where Ember is they'll let her watch the TV. She would be so proud of me. Jenny Jones was always her favorite. She always said she loved to hate the people that came on there, but surely she wouldn't feel that way about me. Luster wouldn't be proud of me, though. He used to say that for the average Kentuckian, appearing on a talk show is the summit of human potential. I guess it's downhill for me from here on out.

The first segment went fairly well. I wish they wouldn't have booed Chuck, but I'm thinking the flashing sign up there told them to. Jenny (or Jenny's writers, I reckon) kind of made him out to be some type of villain taking advantage of a sweet little old lady. Dumb-asses. Then they brought out Chuck's daughter from his first marriage. She bitched at both of us, saying how abnormal our relationship was. But I told her she had better shut the fuck up or kiss my ass one, 'cause we're taking care of her baby while she's screwing around in junior high.

The commercial break ends and Jenny gets her cue.

"Hi. We're back talking to Chuck and Opal, a newly-wed couple who claim to have a deep love for each other despite the fact that he's twenty-nine and she's eighty-one.

We have time for a few questions from the audience."

She goes over to hold the microphone to the big mouth of a big woman.

"This question goes to the long-haired, bearded dude."

"That's Chuck," says Jenny.

"Right. This question is for Chuck. Get a life. She's not active like you are. Get someone else."

I say, "By God, listen here, you big-popoed hoochie," but Chuck grabs my thigh with authority and interrupts my butt.

"Let me tell you something, she *is* active. I have loved a whole lot o' women, but there ain't nothin like ridin down the highway about 90 miles an hour with this woman on the back of my scooter."

The audience laughs, and Chuck takes my hand and gives it a love squeeze. The next question comes from a big fat black lady.

"This question is also for Chuck. That is the only mother you're ever gonna have. You should love your mother."

"That doesn't apply at all to this situation," says Jenny. "Opal and Chuck are husband and wife."

"Oh, well, in that case, you should date people your own age. That's just weird."

"Hey now!" says Chuck, but this time there's no stopping me. I interrupt him.

"Listen, woman. Eat me, and while you're at it, eat shit and die, fuck-wad." The censors are gonna have to beep the fuck out of me.

"Secondly, there's no pleasing you people. All my life people have been asking me, 'Why don't you get married?,' 'Why do you want to be an old maid?,' 'Why do you have so many sex toys in your old age?' Well, here I am. I've finally settled down and married. I even got a granddaughter I take care of for that little slut." I point to Chuck's daughter, Cheyenne.

"Sure Chuck's young, and I'm old, but is it impossible for y'all to believe that we could be happy? In all that's happened in this world, couldn't something as little as that be possible? Can't y'all get past it? Well, if you can't, y'all just wait 'til you're this old, and you'll be past everything. Besides, look at him. Can you blame me?"

Chuck instinctively knows that he's been cued to stand up and shake his fanny for the crowd. He's got on his painted-on jeans, Metallica T-shirt, and a blue jean vest, and the ladies yell "Woo!" when they catch a glimpse of his perfect duff.

"That ain't for y'all," he says. "That's for her. That's all hers."

"So Opal, is Chuck just a sex object to you?" asks Jenny.

"More like she's *my* sex object," says Chuck. After the audience is done groaning, I answer Jenny's question.

"No, Jenny. I mean, sure, he rattles my bones and he's got a great backside, but he's more than just a sex object. He's kind of like my savior."

"How so?" Jenny asks.

"Well, he came into my life at a time when I really needed somebody. My band had just fallen apart, and everything sucked, and I was gettin so I didn't really want to live anymore. I gave up on hope. When my trampy nieces and my therapist were still wanting to put me in a nursing home, I finally got so I didn't even put up a fight."

"But then she met me," interrupts my husband.

"Yeah. Then I met Chuck. He was the orderly at the

nursing home, and it wasn't long before he moved me out of that home, and then we shacked up, and now we're hitched for eternity, and I love this boy."

He kisses my hand, and the audience goes "Ahh." Chuck puts his hunky, tattooed arm around me, and I pat him on the leg. I reckon these people going "Ahh" is the closest thing to acceptance that we're gonna get, even if a flashing sign told them to do it.

"Wait, Jenny. Jenny, I'd like to say something, Jenny," says my excited Chuck.

"Go right ahead," says Jenny.

"Hell, *she* saved *me*, too. Before I met this woman, all I cared about was stealing old people's medication. I'd tell 'em I was Jesus, and they'd just hand their pills right over. I just wanted to be messed up all the time. Now I'm all messed up on this woman's love." We get ahhs and applause.

So everybody's saving everybody. Just like I told that ol' gay boy Kip and the others last week, people need people. Everybody's got a void to fill. Mine had been building up all my life, longer than I could remember, and it was my own fault. I was taking everything too seriously. But now I'm to where I don't care if you're a funny-actin black boy or a long-haired orderly or some sexy alien creature. I just don't care anymore. If you can fill my void, I'll fill yours.

Child

Opal ended up making it farther than any of us. She is on TV. I'm not supposed to be watching TV.

Opal finally found a man. They're beeping her. She visits me sometimes. The housemother bitch doesn't like her. She thinks Opal is a bad influence. Sometimes she tells Opal I'm not here when I am.

One of my roommates named Amber comes in. She sits next to me on the floor. We both sit Indian style. She's dressed just like me like the dress code says to. I must look like a dork.

"Hey. That woman with the poofy white hair used to be my babysitter," I say.

"Shut up, Ember. You are such a liar."

"Kiss my ass."

"Make me."

"*Make me?* You are *so* obvious," I tell her. "And then I say, 'I don't make trash, I burn it,' right? Right?!"

She doesn't answer. I growl at her and throw the remote control at her head but miss.

I shouldn't be so mean to the other girls. Lots of us have the same stories. Amber's mom used to give her Nyquil every afternoon. Then Amber would say, "Mommy, I am so sleepy," and her mom would laugh at her.

"I was in a band with that lady. We played a show. But we broke up after our keyboard guitarist was shot."

"All you ever do is *lie!*"

Our old bitch of a housemother comes in yelling.

"Girls! Stop that bickering! You shouldn't even be watching TV. It is not TV time. It is play time. You should be playing in your room."

"It's not even play time. It's study time," I say.

"Don't talk back to me. You should be in your room memorizing your words. Go to your room, now!"

Amber obeys and runs off to our room. I keep watching TV.

"Ember, I'm not going to tell you again. Go to your room."

I pretend like I don't hear her. I keep watching TV.

"Ember, if you don't start being more obedient and follow the rules of this home, I *will* call your parents."

"They moved to Cancun! What are they gonna do to me? Go ahead and call them."

"I *said* don't talk back to me, young lady! What are you doing watching that filth, anyway?"

"My friend is on there."

"Didn't I just say not to talk back to me?"

"You asked me a question, dumb-ass."

"Watch your mouth! Oh, it's that Oglesby lady."

Opal is on TV again. Her husband is holding her back from attacking the audience.

"We don't watch that kind of trash in this house."

The dumb bitch turns off the TV.

"Burn in hell," I tell her. I stare at her. I want to hurt her and others like her and everyone.

"Don't you try to scare me, you little brat. Go to your room, or I'll give you a beating worse than your parents ever could've."

I give her the meanest look possible. Then I walk up the stairs. I hear her turn the TV back on. I hear Jerry Springer. I creep back down the stairs.

She lights a cigarette and sits down to watch. I crawl back into the room to behind her chair. I pull out a lighter of my own. I light the bottom of her pants leg. Her pants are on fire before she even knows what's happened to her.

Sister

Before I go off, I have some unfinished business at the old Ken's Fried Chicken. Remembering how lascivious David can be, I button up the top button of my blouse before I enter. I don't want to tempt him.

I don't know the girl at the counter, but I'm sure David hired her since she's got that slutty way about her, the same way I suppose I have as well.

"Can I take your order?" she asks.

"Is David Silver here?"

"No. He's in jail. He got busted for selling crack. Why?"

"Oh. I—well, my friend and I stole from him a while back, and I wanted to apologize and give him the money we owed him. But I guess I'll just eat some chicken instead." I'm relieved I don't have to see him and glad that he got his. Sorry, but I am.

I take my seat and self-consciously eat my chicken. I realize that sadly, sitting all alone eating a Commander's Crispy Bits Deal in this depressing Ken's Fried Chicken will be the last supper I have in civilization for a long time. I had always hoped that by the time I was no longer a teenager (I'm twenty now) I would be able to do things like eat alone in public yet not feel awkward or pathetic. But it still bothers me, which is why I don't really mind when a prettyboy struts up to me after dumping his tray.

"Whuzup?" he says.

"Hi," I say as I notice he's wearing more jewelry than I. Three earrings and three necklaces. Plus a goatee and highlights in his hair.

"Weren't you in that band?"

"The Anomalies?"

"Yeah. You guys were tight. Can I sit with you?"

"Please do." I decide to be as affable as possible in these moments before he hits on me. "I can't believe you remember us! It was like a year ago and we only played one song at the one show we had."

"Yeah. But, shit, that was a pretty memorable show, you know whum sayin?"

"Yeah."

"It's a shame your keyboard guitarist got shot like that. Is he okay?"

"Yeah, he is. Thanks for asking. It wasn't that serious of a wound." I should say that at least the last time I saw him he was okay. But who knows now. His wife wrote me and warned me to never send him a letter again. He quit writing me, probably because she wasn't giving him any of my replies. She blames us for what happened to Ray. Or rather she blames the capitalized version of "us."

"Everybody liked y'all," remarks the guy.

"Except for that one guy." We laugh together.

"Yeah. I liked you a lot, though. I'm normally not into that kind of music, you know whum sayin, but I still liked it."

"Thank you. What kind of music *are* you into?"

"All kinds...I especially liked you, you know? Everybody was like, 'Man, that is the hottest drummer *ever*.'"

Here we go again. Again we go here.

"Thanks."

"Any chance of a reunion show so I can watch you beating on those things again?"

"I'm afraid not. Everyone's gone a separate way." And our ways could not be more separate. One of us is on the opposite side of the world. Two of us have been quarantined by the powers that be. I've prepared to quarantine myself. I used to see Opal occasionally, but she was always with her husband, and I'm not about to hang around him again. The last time I visited, he made a pass at me when Opal left the room.

"Well, maybe you could give me a private show. I'd love to see you beat those things again."

"Sorry. I sold my drums."

"That's too bad. Go out with me later. We could go grind at a club and do some body shots."

"I'm a nun."

It's the best excuse for rejecting guys that I've ever come up with and works especially well since it's the truth. Well, I'm still in the novitiate period, but I'm positive I'll take my vows. The others already refer to me as "sister," and my mother superior said it's okay to call myself a nun.

"Whoa. No way."

"Honest to God. Come on. I know you had been noticing my cross."

I hold up the simple wooden crucifix that had been resting atop my chest.

"So? I'm wearing one of those, too." He separates one of his necklaces from the others, one with an ornate gold cross on it. I pull out my Sisters of Bathsheba ID card, one that I carry around for situations like this.

"See. Sister Aurora Buchanan. I'm actually leaving for Mandocello Mount this afternoon. I'm gonna be cloistered."

"But—I—You're so hot, and you were putting out those vibes. Are you screwing with me?"

I have to laugh.

"No. I'm telling you the truth. But I've got a lot of crap from the other sisters for those 'vibes' as you call them. I don't care, though. This is how I look, this is how I dress. I think how I look is a permanent phase."

"Amen." I can tell by the look on his face that he's having trouble dealing with the concept of an enticing nun. "So did you get the calling?"

"No. That's what all the other nuns say, though. For me, it just seemed like the thing for a girl like me to do. After that show you saw, everything kind of went to hell. I lost my friends, my father ran off with a stripper, and I lost my faith in everything.

"So then I started dating a lot to keep from being lonely, which was stupid in the first place, because what's wrong with being lonely? Anyhow, I dated a bunch of handsome morons, and when I wouldn't put out, they kept saying, why don't you go be a nun? So I went and became a nun."

As he nods along to what I'm saying, I think he's starting to believe that I really am a nun. I'm sure it's hard for a guy to swallow. He can accept it and feel ashamed about trying to get in the pants of a woman married to God, or he can continue to pursue me, thinking how cool it would be to do a nun and then tell his friends.

"Oh, man. I sure am sorry, Sister. Is it a sin to hit on a nun?"

I'm genuinely surprised that he said this and smile at him sweetly and sexlessly.

"I don't really know if it's a sin, but just in case, you should probably go home and take a cold shower to wash it away."

He apologizes again, gets up, says good-bye, and leaves me alone.

Criminal

My tiny dick and I never had a chance in this world. I should have been born right here in the human zoo. This is where I belong, the perfect place to finish out my unsuccessful socialization.

But this is not crappily ever after. My body is cramped and confined, but my mind still wears a Parisian nightsuit and waltzes down a suburban street in Buffalo. And that is not even my greatest triumph. The grace that saves me is this—*I like it here*.

People have been my problem all along. Here they cannot get to me. I am free from all the humanoids following each other around in circles, putting things off as long as they can, not expecting anything from life. I like it here where I belong. I rock it inward, outward, and onward.

The other inmates do not play with my ass because they think I am so weird. There are no more nightmare days because I am not aware when the sun is up. I do not miss the sun. The sun is just another star, and we are what makes it special. I pity the sun.

When they let me out of here, I hope to get sent back as quickly as possible. As Fyodor Dostoyevsky wrote, "All great men or even men a little out of the common…must from their very nature be criminals…Otherwise, it's hard for them to get out of the common rut." I want my crimes to be creative. Maybe they will even make me big and famous.

The only thing I miss about the world is being with those few strays that loved me. But I have not kept in touch with them, nor do I plan to. I do not want to know how they spend their days because it might not match up with what is in my head. So I will be content in assuming that Opal is still a maneater senior, breaking hearts of all ages, staying young and free. I am sure that Ray is still enjoying this country more than the ingrates that were born here. I figure Ember finally ran away from her parents and that she will remain a happy runaway forevermore, entirely free from Those Who Know Best. And I see Aurora remaining slutty yet chaste, not giving anything up to anybody.

I have peace in knowing that wherever they are, what is left of the human spirit rocks defiantly in them. And for that, it is an honor to pay for their mistakes, here where I belong, where I hear the guard coming my way.

"Johnson! For the last time, stop talking to yourself, you crazy crackhead!" he says.

Oh no. I am no crackhead. My brain was fried from the second I was born, not by drugs but by everyone I ever met. But I have been trying to recover in here. For a person like me, life is the struggle of getting back what other people's eyeballs have taken away. The greatest ideal that any of us can hope for is to be able to see the world the way it looks in a blind man's dream.

"Who said that?"

I said that.

"Yeah, but who said it first? I mean, you're always quoting those old authors."

That is just something I do to show people that I am not as dumb as I look. That quote was all mine. I was saying something completely new for a change.

"No wonder it didn't make sense. Quiet down, would ya?"

Fine. I will just listen to some rock music.

"Whatever." The guard leaves me.

Alone I dance in a way that probably looks ridiculous to music that only I can hear.

Author

The plot has been contrived and tied in proper knots, its protagonists put in their place, themes thoroughly scoured, every point of view painstakingly encompassed, all symbols self-consciously struck, irony choked dry, and emotion and humor swollen complete, though yet to be addressed is the condition of a significant portion of the publication's inhabitants, those characters which our rejected dreamer Luster Johnson would refer to as "humanoids," the stereotypical commoners collectively representing our antagonist.

Nothing happened to them.

These crude representatives of the satisfied masses, the obsequious settlers for less, continued down the pig-tailed path which their progenitors set out on before them, foraging around rather than forging ahead, scavenging to satisfy the basest of human desires, hating and loving for socially manufactured incentives presented by natural boundaries of land and flesh, artlessly doing, getting, coming and going, competing instead of creating, living so similarly, behaving identically, poorly dancing in unison to the same old sad song because the routine comes to them as easily and as naturally as breathing oxygen, as breast feeding, as reading left to right.

This is not to say our faceless antagonists did not live happily after fulfilling their supporting roles in this work, though "contentedly" would probably be the more appropriate modifier, and it should also be noted that the high-light of their lives, as suggested by their very presence in this publication, was their brushes with our five individuals who not only personify the infinite possibilities inherently granted to the mind that thinks freely, but who also insinuate the idea that potential greatness rises not so much from an affection or even fondness for fellow man, but rather a disdain, for it is a disgusted, not enamored individual who rises from the aforementioned masses to better the world, that is if this unconventional individual's contempt is balanced with just enough love to devote a damn for fellow man, and provided that such an anomalous being would be allowed to entertain his or her senseless thoughts by those of us who can't help but to rely on oxygen, who can't help but to find nourishment in breasts, who can't help but to read from left to right. Freed and discovered be can individual this hope only can we.

Acknowledgments

These are the people I will never be able to thank enough:

My mother, Nancy, and my sister, CeCe, who know me better than anyone ever will and still love me. I want you both to be happy more than anything.

Pat Walsh, who has taken the risk of believing in me, as well as David Poindexter and everyone else who plays on the MacAdam/Cage softball team with me.

Michael Bruner, the Dillinghams, the Walkers, and Rene and John for the love, generosity, and encouragement they've shown my family and me for so long.

All of my teachers, especially those English teachers by the names of Craig Barrette, David Bartholomy, Vicki Combs, Ellen Dugan-Barrette, and Susie Thurman.

And all of those who I grew up with in Henderson, Kentucky, who have laughed with me, and especially those who have laughed at me.